# AN
# INDECENT
# PROPOSAL

J.C. REED

&

JACKIE STEELE

Cover art by Larissa Klein

Editing by Shannon Wolfman

ISBN: 1508543259
ISBN-13: 978-1508543251

## ABOUT AN INDECENT PROPOSAL

It was supposed to be easy.

Hire a professional actor to play my fake fiancé.

But when he steps in front of my door to pick me up for The Interview, my heart stops. Chase Wright is perfect. And hot. I mean like 'burn up your dress hot.' However, Chase isn't professional at all. I hate what he does to me with his sinfully sexy blue eyes. I hate that he wants me in his bed.

One month...that's all I need him for. All I have to do is stay out of his bed.

But the rules slowly begin to change. My fake fiancé suddenly becomes my fake husband. When Chase offers me an indecent proposal, it's too late to fire him.

It's too late to decline.


Includes free prequel novella THAT GUY.

# THAT GUY

OUT OF ALL the dates in my life, Tuesday at 10 a.m. was about the worst time disaster could strike. I was sitting in the waiting area of LiveInvent Designs—the one place where I had been dying to get an interview since finishing college.

Apart from me, nineteen other graduates were waiting for their big chance, all dressed in immaculate, tailored business suits—the kind I couldn't afford. But what I couldn't offer in expensive clothes, I knew I could make up in hard work and dedication. I was a professional, and as such I was determined to make a good impression.

"Lauren Hanson?"

I straightened up in my seat and smiled as one of the personal assistants called my name. "Yes." I stood and took a deep breath, waiting for further instructions.

"Please take the elevator up to the thirtieth floor. Someone will be expecting you."

*The thirtieth floor.*

According to LiveInvent's website, it was the place where the big-shot strategists worked. Los Angeles wasn't just home to some of the greatest marketing companies in the United States; it was also the best place to get started and to experience an environment of "what if," not just "if only."

When I applied for a graduate position as a marketing assistant, I had never even considered the possibility that one of them might like my resume enough to want to meet me personally. But now it was happening.

My dream was coming true.

I brushed my hands over my gray skirt nervously and with measured steps made my way to the elevator area, ignoring the people ambling up and down the corridor in their immaculate expensive clothes, seemingly oblivious to the outside world. They were probably used to their simple yet sophisticated surroundings, with marble floors and beautiful peonies, and calla lilies arranged in crystal centerpieces. The walls were adorned with polished frames displaying awards and the company's most successful

4

projects showcased like little trophies.

I stopped in front of the elevators, and sighed happily. This wasn't just any workplace—it was heaven. And I wanted to be a part of it. Whatever it took.

This was my dream.

It *had* to come true.

A bell chimed, and one of the three elevator doors opened, giving me a view of a small but tastefully decorated space. Soft music was playing in the background at a pleasant volume. As I stepped into the small elevator, I bumped into someone.

It happened so quickly: my CV folder slipped out of my hands and dropped to the floor. I squatted to reach for the folder when I noticed the pair of black, expensive slacks. I raised my eyes slowly, taking in the custom suit. No, it wasn't so much the suit, but more the tall height, his black hair, his broad shoulders, the sexy male fragrance he was wearing, that drew my attention to him.

His Rolex suggested that he wasn't an applicant. Probably an executive.

Before I knew it, the bell chimed again. I rose to my feet quickly before the doors closed again.

I pressed the backlit button embossed with the number thirty. No need to check him out, not when I didn't know if he wasn't an interviewer. Getting the job was more important than checking out the next hot guy.

I turned my back on him, and mentally recollected my primed answers to possible interview questions.

*Breathe in, breathe out.*

This was it…my big chance.

All my life I had worked hard for this exact day. Just a few more seconds. And then I would give it all my best, because I just had to have this job.

There was no possibility, no other option, no what-ifs.

If I wanted to make it in the business world and get out of my outstanding debt, I had to go the extra mile. I was ready—more than ever because any other outcome wasn't an option.

My hands turned clammy from my increasing nervousness, and my mouth went a little dry. I was so absorbed in my thoughts that I didn't register that the elevator had stopped moving until a little shake told me something was up. I looked up from the floor, only to see we had stopped at the twenty-ninth floor, and the doors had remained closed.

Seriously? Did we *have* to stop one floor below my destination?

I raised my eyebrows when the guy behind me began to press the buttons on the control panel in an impatient manner. The music was gone, plunging us into eerie silence.

Frowning, I turned to face him, wondering what the heck was going on, but all I caught were blue eyes just before the bulbs started to flicker. The lights flashed once more, then switched off, bathing us in complete darkness.

"What the—" I heard him cussing, his deep voice filled with annoyance.

For a moment, I held my breath, my heart pounding in my chest as I waited for the lights to switch on again. A few seconds passed, which turned into minutes. And still there was no light, no movement—nothing to indicate we even were in an elevator.

I blinked in succession, blind in the pitch-black.

As my brain tried to make sense of the situation, countless thoughts began to race through my mind. How long would it take until people noticed there was a technical glitch and sent repairmen? How long were the interviews scheduled to take, and if I appeared late, would I get a second chance? And finally, how long would the oxygen last in such a confined space?

Just theoretically asking.

Not that we were going to be stuck for much longer. Or suffocate anytime soon, because that would be a worst-case scenario. But it would only be natural to know…just in case.

I wasn't claustrophobic—actually, far from it. But dark, enclosed spaces weren't exactly my favorite place to be. And particularly not those with no clear exit sign. The minutes continued to fly until I was sure we had been in there for at least twenty minutes. Or maybe it just felt that way.

I sighed impatiently.

"There must be an assistance button," I said as I let my fingers brush over the cold steel wall. My hand touched his, and an electric jolt ran through me. I pulled back nervously.

"Sorry," I whispered.

"No problem."

In the silence around us, I could hear his finger pressing buttons every other second, as if that would make someone hurry faster. At last, the stranger let out a frustrated sigh. Something rustled, followed by shuffling.

I narrowed my gaze to focus in the pitch darkness, but my vision didn't sharpen to allow me to see contours.

Nothing stood out.

I groaned and braced myself against the feeling of helplessness growing inside me. Not seeing anything while knowing there was no window or door I could open was already scary. Combine that with the fact that I had no idea if help was on its way, and the entire situation was turning into a nightmare scenario.

The guy was probably just as frustrated as I was, because I heard him shifting.

"What are you doing?" I asked as more rustling sounds carried over from the floor.

"Trying to find my cell." His voice came from beneath

me, which made me figure at some point he must have kneeled down—or assumed a sitting position.

I wet my lips nervously.

A stranger was doing God only knew what at my feet. Now that made it hard to ignore him.

For a moment, I considered joining him, and then the word "cell" registered in my mind. Of course! A phone was the answer to my prayers.

"Shit. It's not here. I must have left it in the car." He exhaled another frustrated sigh. "Do you have yours?"

"Not on me." Which was kind of the truth. The day before, my handbag, together with my purse and cell phone, had been stolen. Lucky for me, my credit cards were maxed out to the limit, and my pre-paid cell had both a lock and no minutes, so the loss was minimal.

"Okay." His tone was surprisingly calm as he drew out the word. "Let's see if the emergency phone's working."

I jumped back as his hand reached over my chest, almost touching the thin fabric of my top.

"Hello?" he asked. Silence fell. Holding my breath, I strained to listen. The line remained dead. No voice, no white noise, nothing to indicate anyone had been alerted to our situation.

My heart began to thump hard against my ribcage, and a thin rivulet of sweat rolled down my back as realization kicked in that it might take a while before someone was alerted.

"Can you try again?" My voice came so thin and raspy, I knew I was close to having a panic attack.

"No point. Phone's not working. Reception's gone. We're stuck," the guy said, almost bored. No panic. No whining. Just cool composure with a hint of an annoyance, as if the entire situation was a mere inconvenience he experienced on a regular basis. Unlike me, he seemed to breathe just fine.

He sighed. "Let's hope they won't close off the elevator area for the rest of the day," he said to himself with…humor?

I swallowed hard.

If that was true, and we ended up stuck in there all day, we'd never last. We'd run out of oxygen and—

Come to think of it, didn't I read somewhere that people could die within two hours when stuck in a confined space? And hadn't we already been stuck for some time?

A sense of foreboding settled in the pit of my stomach.

Something was wrong. Very wrong. I could feel it in the oppressive silence and the fact that the stranger had stopped pressing buttons and rummaging through his pockets. The air was getting increasingly hot, making it hard to breathe. The rivulet turned into a layer of sweat covering my entire back as I tried to force oxygen into my lungs.

In that moment, a loud thud reverberated from the

walls, followed by a short, faint shrill.

An alarm?

*Oh, my god.*

This wasn't some technical glitch. It was a real-life emergency. Something had happened. Something really bad. Faintly, I could hear hurried steps, some of them pounding, but none of them seemed to stop near the elevators. Everyone would forget about the two people stuck in the elevator, because they had more pressing issues to attend to—like saving themselves. The alarm continued to blare in the distance.

To my utter shock, a whimper escaped my throat as fear consumed me.

"Oh, God." My voice came high-pitched, reflecting the dark thought that kept circling in my mind.

*I'm going to die.*

The thought hit me so hard a wave of dizziness rushed over me. But, at twenty-two, I was too young for my demise, particularly because I hadn't even started to live my life yet. I had struggled through college while amassing a vast student loan debt that had kept me strapped for cash for years.

How ironic would it be if the one job I had thought would be the answer to my prayers might just kill me?

The thought of being stuck in a confined space, missing the most important interview of my life while dying from oxygen depletion, was too much. Suddenly, my breathing quickened, and my pulse began to race hard and fast.

I realized the whizzing sound echoing in my ears wasn't a result of my frayed nerves but a noise coming out of my mouth.

"I think I'm having a panic attack," I whispered.

"We'll be all right," the guy said, and this time I noticed how smooth and deep his voice was.

Sexy, with the slightest hint of a rumble to it.

Maybe my other senses were sharpened in the darkness, or we were indeed running out of oxygen and my brain was slowly starting to play tricks on me, but in the confined space I could smell him clearly. Not just his aftershave, but *him*—the man who couldn't see me. The only person who would witness my untimely death.

"I'm not sure." I choked on my voice. "What if no one comes?"

"What's your name?" Sexy Voice said.

"Lauren, but everyone calls me Laurie," I whispered.

Something warm brushed my shoulder, instantly raising goose bumps across my arm, and trailed down my arm until it touched my hand. Strong fingers clasped around my hand and squeezed, not hard enough to hurt me, but the motion helped me regain some of my composure, and make me realize that I wasn't alone.

"Okay, Laurie. This is likely just a temporary glitch. You

need to calm down."

I *was* calm, wasn't I?

I'd opened my mouth to tell him that when the air whizzed out of my lungs in a hot *swoosh*. It sounded like someone was whistling, and not in a pretty way. And there I had thought it was the sound of the elevator, when it had been me all along.

"I can't," I whispered. "I can't breathe. I feel like I'm choking."

To my dismay, I started shaking and my breathing came faster.

"You're hyperventilating," Sexy Voice said, increasing the pressure of his grip. "I need you to breathe with me. Okay, Laurie?" He inhaled and exhaled deeply, his hot breath caressing my skin, and I realized just how close he was standing. Under normal circumstances, too close for comfort.

Only, these weren't normal circumstances.

Staring blindly ahead, I followed his instructions, inhaling with him, holding my breath, and then exhaling again.

"Are you feeling better?" he asked.

I shook my head, even though he couldn't see me, as tears pricked the corners of my eyes.

"We can't even call for help. If we're stuck in here for a whole day, we'll die," I whispered.

"No." His tone was sharp. Defiant. "People know we're in here. Security is calling for help this instant."

"You don't know that," I muttered.

"Trust me. I do."

I wanted to believe him so badly my whole body hurt from the effort. But, for some reason, his words rang empty and senseless. "People can die in elevators. I read about it last week."

"Not us. Not today." His hands began to rub up and down my arms, as though to soothe me, but the motion only managed to send a layer of ice down my spine.

For a while, we just stood there, rivulets of sweat running down my spine. The whole space, as small as it was, had the temperature of a sauna.

"It's so hot," I whispered. "I really can't breathe."

"You can do it, Laurie. Focus on my voice. Focus on taking slow, deep breaths through your nose, and exhale through your mouth. That's all that matters now. Nothing else."

I forced more air into my lungs, but even though oxygen reached my brain, somehow it didn't have the desired calming effect on me. "The funny thing is, I'm not ready to die," I said weakly, squeezing his hands for support.

"You won't." His determined tone left no room for discussion. "Tell me something about yourself." He was trying to divert my attention from the situation at hand, only it didn't work. "Where do you live? What do you like doing in your free time?"

"There's nothing to tell. I'm boring."

A sexy little laugh, then, "I highly doubt that, Laurie. You sound like an interesting person."

In spite of myself, I smiled. He had no idea how wrong he was. "No, really. I'm a bore."

"Well, try me. I'm in no hurry."

Neither was I. We'd probably been stuck for more than two hours, and I needed a distraction.

"Laurie," he prompted, hesitating. Or maybe he was having trouble breathing as well. And then I noticed it: a slight shaking and vibrating of the walls. It stopped almost as quickly as it had started.

His hands let go of me. Clothes rustled, and something dropped to the floor with a muffled thud. Then his hands were back on me, his bare skin brushing mine in the process, his fingers holding mine.

I realized he must have taken off his jacket and rolled up his sleeves. The air was getting hot. It wasn't just my imagination. Suddenly, I had a vision of dying without clearing my conscience. If I couldn't do all the things I had envisioned I'd be doing with my life, if I died and all the things about heaven and hell were true, then I needed to at least relieve my conscience.

Confess.

Acknowledge my mistakes to find absolution.

Well, you get the point.

"You think I'm interesting?" I asked, not waiting for his answer. "Okay, I'll tell you something about me. I have five secrets. Five secrets I don't want to carry with me to the grave. Probably the only five things that don't render me a complete bore."

"You're being melodramatic. It's just a technical glitch. People are—"

"Coming to rescue us. Yeah, got it." I rolled my eyes because I didn't believe a word he said. "Except that it sure felt like an earthquake, and everyone's probably gone."

"Earthquakes happen all the time. And people return for those left behind. So, what are your secrets?"

The air was getting all hot and stuffy because the air conditioning was no longer working. Already my lungs were burning, and my head was dizzy. It was only a matter of time until we ran out of oxygen, and he knew it.

"You want to hear them? Well, I'm scared of dark places. Any dark place," I said. "Always have been, and this is my worst nightmare."

"You don't need to be scared. I'm here. Being stuck in an elevator is not a big deal. And a lot of people are scared of the dark, but once you know it's just in your mind, your imagination, your fear talking, you'll get over it."

I smiled bitterly. "You're great at this. You really are.

And if I had to go through this all over again and I could choose one person to be stuck in an elevator with, it'd probably be you. But that doesn't change anything. I'm still scared out of my mind. It's—"

"Nyctophobia."

"Yeah, that."

In the darkness, I could feel the smile on his lips, and for a moment I took the time to imagine him. But all that came out was a fuzzy picture of blue eyes and a soft, sexy smile.

Maybe lopsided.

Or dimples, because I was a sucker for those.

"What's number two?" His voice was hoarse now. Definitely trouble breathing.

"I'm buried in student and credit card loans. It's so bad, it's unreal. Last week I said to my best friend Jude that if I didn't get this interview, I'd fake my resume just to get a job. Any job. She laughed about it, but I meant it. I'm really that desperate."

"The depravity of it," Sexy Voice said. Was he mocking me? I had just opened my mouth to speak with a comeback burning on the tip of my tongue when he cut me off. "I think, given the circumstances, it's understandable. It doesn't make you a bad person...unless you pretend to be a dentist. My point is, there's far worse out there."

"Probably." I sucked in a deep breath and regretted it

instantly. My head felt so dizzy, I feared I might just pass out. I had to hurry up if I wanted to get to the highlight of my little confession.

"I guess we all revert to lying and cheating if we want to achieve something, because there's no other way to get there. What about the next one?" Sexy Voice said, as though reading my mind.

"You're not bored yet?"

"Not yet. It's definitely getting interesting." His fingers brushed my wrist, and in spite of the macabre of the situation, I found myself relishing his touch, maybe enjoying it a bit more than was proper.

The next point on my little list was a little tricky. "I'm twenty-two, and yet I'm a virgin," I said before I could stop myself.

"Maybe you never found find the right person, or the right situation," he whispered after a slight pause.

I laughed, fighting the need to elaborate. "You have an excuse for everything, don't you?"

"I'm just a realist."

"Or an optimist." With a sexy voice, and a sexy body, and a face I couldn't remember. Too bad we were about to suffocate, or else I might have found myself just a little bit drawn to this one.

The darkness before my eyes began to spin. If it weren't for his strong arms around me, I would have dropped to the floor, too weak to sit up straight. "I might need to cut to the last point on my list," I said. "And it's a big one. I have carried it all my life."

"Hold on to me," he whispered.

I was. More than he'd ever know.

"Someone died because of me." My voice came so low and faint, I wasn't sure he could hear me. "I'll never be able to live with myself."

Silence. For a second, I wondered if he had even heard me.

"I'm sure it wasn't like that. It was an accident," he said at last.

No hesitation.

No blame.

No mistrust.

Either he was a good person and believed in the good in people, or he was trying to keep the conversation light because of our situation, and then sprint for the nearest exit—if we ever made it out alive.

I shook my head. "You don't know me. You know nothing about me."

Another pause. A few seconds passed, during which I could hear his breathing, slow and steady, but slightly labored.

"Lay down," he whispered. "The air's cooler on the floor."

Didn't he hear what I'd just told him? He tugged at my hand, and I did as instructed.

His arms wrapped around me and he drew me to his chest. I nestled in his arms.

The minutes passed, and the alarm continued to blare. With every second, breathing became harder. If out of a lack of oxygen or something else, I couldn't tell.

"No one's coming for us, are they?" I whispered inaudibly, my face buried against his strong chest. He smelled so good it was impossible to resist his scent.

"We should do something to take our mind off it," he whispered. His voice had become quiet, shaky, heavy, and—was that fear?

"What?"

"I could kiss you," he whispered.

His hands cupped my face. I looked up, my gaze searching him in the darkness, when I realized that this might just be our last moment.

I might die with a stranger.

"Laurie?" he asked, his voice drawing me to reality.

"I don't even know your name," I whispered.

He chuckled. "It doesn't matter now, does it?"

No, not really. "I want to kiss you, too."

In a bold moment, I raised my mouth to meet his. He ran a thumb across my lips before our mouths connected, warm and tender. For a second, I could sense his hesitation, and then his lips opened to claim my mouth with a hunger that took my breath away.

The sound of an alarm continued to carry over, but I didn't care. All I wanted were this stranger's lips on mine and the hot waves of want he sent through me, helping me to forget, keeping me alive—on the brink of sanity—with nothing but a kiss. I had never felt this way before. I had never been in such a state of fear and gratitude that I wasn't alone. Then again, I had never been so close to dying.

My fingers tangled in his hair, pulling him closer, our mouths meeting once more, when something hard crashed against the walls, resulting in a loud thud. I turned my head toward the door.

A shrill noise, like metal scratching against metal, echoed, followed by the sound of a different alarm, the noise increasing in volume. I pressed my palms against my ears, and watched how something pried the door open.

"They're here for us," I said, relief streaming through me. He didn't say anything.

"Did you hear what I just said?" I asked again, touching him. "You were right. They came back for us."

Suddenly, a bright light blinded me. I raised my hand to shield my eyes from the blinding brightness.

Arms wrapped around me and pulled me to my feet, and something cold was pressed against my face. I inhaled automatically, then with more fervor as I realized someone was holding an oxygen mask against my mouth and nose.

"I've got her," a male voice yelled in my ear, the sound almost as loud as the blaring in the background. "We're coming out now."

My head snapped back toward the elevator, in the stranger's direction, and I opened my mouth to speak. To my dismay, I realized he wasn't behind me, or maybe I couldn't see him through the thick curtain of charcoal smoke that had filled the hall.

"No. Please help him," I croaked, planting my feet firmly on the ground, but the arms around me were stronger. My voice could barely reach my ears, let alone penetrate the shrill sound of the alarm.

Struggling against the iron grip, I was carried away before I could turn to get a glimpse of the stranger in the elevator. "No," I pleaded. "Please. You've got to help him. Please."

But my voice was too weak to get anyone's attention.

As I was carried down flights and flights of stairs, I glimpsed more people being helped out—their faces reflecting their shock and disbelief. Figuring someone might need it more than I did, I tried to remove the oxygen mask, but my rescuer pressed it against my mouth, his gesture urging me forcefully to keep it on. Eventually we burst through the reception area and onto the street outside, where hundreds of evacuated office workers and onlookers had gathered, some filming the event on their cell phones, others commenting loudly.

"I'm fine," I said to a concerned woman and scanned the faces around me, even though I knew better than to expect a miracle.

My heart was slamming so hard against my chest, I was sure it would break. If the stranger had been rescued, he couldn't possibly find me in the crowd, not least because we hadn't exchanged names. We didn't even know what the other person looked like. As I was guided to the waiting medical assistance, a crashing sound rang behind me so loud that the rumble rocked my body and the ground beneath my feet vibrated. A cloud of dust billowed into the sky.

My heart stopped.

"The library," a woman in the crowd shouted. "It's the library. It's gone."

"The whole floor's collapsed."

"People are still trapped inside," a fireman shouted into what looked like a radio, and began to gesticulate. "Send another unit. I repeat, send another unit. We need as many people as possible."

*Oh, my god.*

I stared at the building, my fingers clasped over my mouth in shock as the disaster unfolded. I didn't know if he had survived, but I hoped he was safe. That he had made it out in time. Chances were slim. I realized if he didn't survive, he'd be my sixth secret—the man with the sexy voice whose name I didn't know.

# AN
# INDECENT
# PROPOSAL

## Chapter 1

*Three months later*

I NEEDED A husband—and fast. Not literally, of course. Just for the weekend, or as long as my stepfather would be in town. A relationship was the excuse I had given for not visiting Waterfront Shore for the last three years. Three years of running away from the place of my dreams and nightmares, and a past better left buried forever. And now my lie was catching up with me, because there was no husband or fiancé in sight, not even a boyfriend or a date to play the part.

"Hire an actor," said Jude, who was looking up from her computer screen. "In fact, he's perfect." She jumped up and headed over to me, her chiffon dress revealing long, tanned legs as she sat down on the sofa and tucked her legs beneath her. I stared open-mouthed at the half-naked model on the screen. He looked hot, no doubt about it, but he also looked—

"Desperate," I mumbled to myself.

"I wouldn't exactly call you 'desperate.' More like 'inventive' or—"

"Thanks," I muttered, cutting her off. "But I was talking about the guy."

For a moment we remained silent as I read the text beneath the picture of a man with a strong chin, dark brown hair, and eyes the color of an ocean shimmering in the sunlight, a shade of eye color I'd never seen before. I figured it was either Photoshopped, or they were contact lenses, which only managed to fortify my first impression of him.

Desperate. Plain desperate.

And his description in his own words didn't help improve his image, either.

*Chase is a very nice, humorous, and down-to-earth lover of female beauty. He knows how to cook and offers to carry things when shopping.*

"He sounds dreamy," Jude gushed.

I fought the urge to roll my eyes at her. "He sounds like a bellboy with playboy aspirations. Either that, or he's a crook waiting for gullible women to fall for his creepy charm. I bet the profile's fake."

Oblivious to my sarcasm, or maybe she was just ignoring me, Jude picked up the phone and dialed the number in his contact details. I stared at her, not believing that she was going for it. I figured she'd come to her senses the moment she heard the guy's voice, which I imagined was old and cheesy, and even creepier than the fake profile.

"Hey, is that Chase?" Jude held her breath as she listened, then gave me the thumbs-up.

I shook my head in exasperation and dashed for the kitchen to grab a bottle of water, then pressed my back against the cold wall as I forced myself to take slow sips. Maybe Jude had time to waste on yet another one of her usual absurd ideas, but one of us had to keep her feet firmly planted on the ground. Hiring an actor to play my husband wasn't going to happen because it would only backfire.

*Just tell the truth, Hanson. How hard can it be?*

I swallowed.

It wasn't an option. Not even a possibility. If the truth came out, it'd kill me, meaning I'd have to come up with a plan.

"Guess who's got a date tonight," Jude singsonged from the door.

I turned my head wearily to regard her. Her cheeks were flushed, and there was a strange glint in her eyes, like she had just run a few miles, or had marathon sex. She grabbed the water bottle out of my hands and took a swig, then handed it back to me. "Come on, play along."

I shot her a desolate look.

*Please. Let this be a joke.*

"Who?" I asked halfheartedly.

"You, Hanson. Chase is picking you up at seven," she gushed, and I couldn't keep my shoulders from dropping. "You two are going to have dinner, during which you can talk about the job, and, who knows, one thing might just lead to another." She winked, leaving the rest unspoken.

Usually, I would have laughed at her dirty imagination, but right now all I could do was stare at her, open-mouthed. Cold and hot chills ran down my spine at the realization that with *picking up* she actually meant the guy was coming over.

"You gave the creep my home address?" My voice sounded thin, but there was a menacing undertone in it that didn't escape even Jude.

"How else was he supposed to pick you up?" She shrugged defensively, but there was unease in her eyes. "Besides, I didn't give him your real name."

"That's a relief," I said, fighting the urge to shake some much-needed sense into her. "Let's hope he can't read the correct name on the mailbox or ask the concierge. Or remember my face and stalk me home from the grocery store."

"He won't. He sounds like a pretty nice guy." She nodded, probably trying to convince herself as much as me.

Yeah, like sociopaths didn't usually masquerade as nice guys.

I sighed inwardly and changed the topic to more pressing issues.

"All right. How much is he charging for the first hour?" I asked casually. "Surely, if he's a professional actor, he's mentioned his rates."

"Actually"—she looked so guilty I knew she was about to drop the next bomb—"Chase said the first hour is free so you can get to know each other. He's saving you money." Jude beamed. "Isn't he great?"

"It's free?" I said slowly. "Since when is something free? Jude, are you realizing how he sounds? He sounds like a major creep with that little extra killer factor thrown in. Like someone who—"

"I think I got the message," Jude said, cutting me off, her lips pressed into a tight line that reflected her annoyance. I just couldn't figure out if it was aimed at herself or me. "You'll be okay, right, Laurie? If something happens, you'll call me, and I'll come and pick you up."

I laughed darkly. As emergency plans went, calling her was a no-brainer under normal circumstances. However, these weren't exactly normal circumstances. If something bad happened to me…I doubted I'd be able to call while he was busy harvesting my organs and selling them on the black market.

"Besides, he looks too hot to be a madman," she said.

"I guess you're right," I said sarcastically. I should have been angry with Jude for making this hole I had dug myself even deeper, but we had been best friends for a long time. We were never angry at each other—that was the secret of our friendship. Besides, the fear in her eyes told me she realized that she'd made a mistake, one she couldn't wait to rectify.

"Phone him back and call the whole thing off, Jude."

Narrowing her eyes at me, she shook her head vehemently. "No."

"No?" I asked incredulously, realizing the glint in her eyes wasn't one of fear. She was *proud* of her brainless plan and excited to get the ball rolling.

"I've just sorted out all your worries. Just like that." She snapped her manicured fingers in my face. "And you're being an ungrateful little brat. Now, get a life, which you desperately need, Hanson, and start planning your outfit for your date with the most gorgeous guy you—or I, for that matter—have ever seen, because we want to make quite the impression. Come on, we have less than two hours left."

Before I could protest, she grabbed my arm and yanked me after her. I had no choice but to follow, albeit hesitantly, because the prospect of meeting a complete stranger both fascinated and terrified me.

What if he turned out to be completely illiterate? Or arrogant to the point of being a complete ass? I didn't want to have to find a lame excuse to get the hell out of there, because I was the worst liar, and no one ever bought my bluffs.

"I don't want to go." It was a weak attempt at protest, but, truth be told, deep inside I had sort of made the decision long before I even realized it. Jude's plan, as odd and completely absurd as it sounded, was the only option I had at this point. If Chase was only half as good-looking and cultured as he gave the impression in his online profile, and as nice as Jude believed, he might just be fake-fiancé material...if he agreed to play along and didn't kill me in the first place.

"What about this?" Jude retrieved my little black dress and held it up.

I grimaced at her, mortified. "I want to hire him, not bed him."

"Or you could do both," Jude said, grinning.

Jude was a free-spirited soul, but not as free of inhibitions as she liked to pretend to be. Basically, she dated—a lot—but she never jumped into bed with any of the guys, because by the end of the second date she had already found a long list of things to fault, which she hid behind a sparkling smile and a run to the bathroom in order to call me in a desperate attempt to come get her. And every time it was my job to help her out by finding excuses as to why she couldn't see her dates again. It had been like this ever since we met in college and bonded over a watery chai latte served in the café across from her grandparents' townhouse. After telling hundreds of lies to cover for her over the years, I would have expected to be an expert in lying, but fat chance.

Sighing, I threw the dress on the bed and squeezed into a pair of skinny jeans, a black shirt, and a suit jacket that was fitted but covered only half of my butt. Once I'd paired the outfit with flat boots and my fake diamond earrings, and with my hair piled up on my head, I thought I looked modern and fun, but also conservative—yet not too severe to give the impression I might have scared off every guy entering my life, and consequently might be to blame for my current unattached status.

*Unattached status.*

I despised those two words strung together because they sounded like an incurable disease. Given that I was only twenty-three, there was still hope. Unfortunately, some people in my life thought differently, which was why I had fled across the country to be far away from Waterfront Shore. Far away from high expectations and an old life that harbored too many dark secrets.

34

Regarding myself in the floor-to-ceiling mirror, I couldn't help but give an approving nod at my reflection. The jeans emphasized my butt, drawing attention away from the wide hips I used to hate as a teen. The shirt sat tight around my bust, but slightly loose around the waist area so I wouldn't look like a stuffed turkey. And the jacket gave me an academic flair that screamed "business administration professional." I might not be as tall and thin as Jude, or as stunningly pretty, but I knew how to complement my strong points, which were my eyes and my full lips painted in a sheer burgundy red. I was so pleased with my choice of attire that I turned to Jude proudly.

"How do I look?"

"Well, you certainly won't have to fend off any advances, if that's what you're so worried about. It's, simply put, hideous." Jude pointed at my suit jacket, grinning. "You sure you want to wear that? *I* wouldn't hit on you dressed like that."

I turned back to the mirror to give myself a critical once-over. "What's wrong with it?"

"Better ask, what's *not* wrong with it. It reminds me of an eighties music video, and not in a good way."

Jude loved surfing YouTube for old and horrendous music videos. She said it helped with her job as an Internet entrepreneur. After watching her dabble in this and that for the last two years, building websites and blogging, I was still not sure how exactly she was doing it job-wise, but she made more money than I did and paid more than half her share of the bills, so who was I to complain? I loved this jacket and should have felt offended, but the beauty of our friendship was that whatever the other said was accepted as constructive criticism. Given that Jude was also a bit of a fashion fanatic, I knew I should listen to her advice, which I usually did.

Just not today.

"The jacket's staying. End of discussion," I said, and began to apply a thin layer of lipstick. "I'm not meeting this guy to impress him. I'm hiring a professional actor, so he'd better be good and decent. If he so much as looks like a creep, never mind talking or behaving like one, I promise I'll hold you responsible for the rest of your life. After all, it was your idea."

"Relax." Jude laughed. "Tonight isn't just any night. It's your big night."

No idea what she meant by that, and I certainly didn't want to know.

By five to seven, I was more nervous than I cared to admit. I hadn't been on a date in forever. Come to think of it, it had been more than two years. It wasn't from a lack of requests and interest, but more that I was a busy person. There had been college and my search for work, which took up most of my time now.

"I don't think it's a good idea. I don't even have time for Chase," I muttered. His name rolled off my tongue so naturally, it was almost scary. Like it belonged there, with all the implications a sexy male name brought with it.

There, I had said it. He sounded sexy as hell and even looked the part. And we were going to spend time together.

*This isn't a date, Hanson.*

Damn right it wasn't. We were talking a business proposition. A job—if he was half civilized and up for playing the doting fiancé bull. Unfortunately, the knowledge that he was an actor probably desperate to be hired wasn't helping in taking the edge off.

"Hey." Jude snapped her fingers in my face again. I flinched and shot her a WTF look. She glared at me, but there was something strange about her. She was laughing at me, I realized.

Damn it!

Jude knew I was nervous, and she enjoyed every torture-filled second. My cheeks caught fire. I could feel the onset of a blush crawling all over my face and neck, and spreading down to my chest.

To my chagrin, the bell rang and Jude jumped up, dashing for the door before I could stop her.

"Wait. No, Jude." My voice came out all croaky and weak. My heart began to beat so hard I might just be on the verge of having a heart attack. Voices carried over from the hall. Then the tinkle of laughter. Turning toward the open door, I strained to listen. The voices were muffled, but from Jude's eager chatter, I could tell she was delighted and made no secret of it.

*Oh, my god.*

Any moment, I'd have to face him. I turned my head left and right, pondering whether I should maybe climb out the window and just leave. I could always pretend later that I had to pick up some milk and forgot all about the meeting.

"Laurie!" Jude yelled. I flinched and jumped back at the prospect of having been caught eavesdropping. Two pairs of footsteps thumped down the hall. I froze to the spot. She couldn't possibly have asked him—

In they stepped.

I stared in horror at Jude's toned body and then at the brown-haired guy towering behind her, and for a moment the entire situation began to play in slow motion before my eyes. Jude said something, but all I could do was stare at the guy behind her as I broke out in a sweat.

*Fuckety hot!*

That was all my mind could come up with, even though my monosyllabic and simplistic description of him couldn't possibly do him justice.

He was stunning.

I should have been more articulate, but only six words came to my mind straight away.

*Unbelievably stalkable. Fuckably sexy. Simply tastylicious.*

He was so hot he couldn't possibly be real. Perfect in every way, with dark brown hair framing a masculine face with a straight nose, and the kind of bedroom eyes that invited you to gaze into them right before you screamed his name as you came over and over again.

Hell, I wanted to scream his name, and he was probably not even *that* good. I mean, anyone who was physically that flawless must have an ego the size of the White House. The guy's impossibly blue eyes turned on me, and an amused flicker appeared in them. He stepped around Jude with a wicked smile on his lips. My heart dropped in my panties.

*Holy cow.*

He was smiling at me—as if knowing I was attracted to him. That was the last thing I wanted. I forced myself to look away from this impossible beauty, only for my gaze to settle on his chest. Unfortunately, my hormones didn't seem to care much just how unfortunate and awkward the entire situation was.

I wanted to run. I wanted to hide. But all I could do was stay glued to the spot while staring at the way his shirt seemed to emphasize the strong muscles in his arms and draw attention to his flat abdomen and strong thighs. I wondered if they were as hard as they looked.

"Laurie, this is Chase," Jude said, pointing at him. Did I detect a hint of amusement in her voice? And if so, why was everyone laughing at me? Was it that obvious that I was terrified of being alone with this man?

I wanted to say something clever—something that would show him he hadn't turned me into a half-wit—yet. But all I managed was a weak smile. I even found myself holding out my hand, then flinching as he leapt forward and grabbed it in his. I almost shrank back at how warm his skin was.

He had manly hands. Capable but groomed, and I realized in his line of work manicures were probably mandatory. Embarrassed, I pulled back, because, let's be honest, I couldn't remember the last time I had a mani-pedi, but he held on tight, not yet willing to let me go.

"Hi, Laurie."

God, even his voice was perfect.

All deep and sensual, and way too sexy.

He sounded like he had just stepped out of my soft rock iTunes collection. It was the kind of voice that urged a woman to dream of places far away from her office. Places that might end up with him being in my bed. And what woman with her panties in the right place wouldn't be attracted to that? Besides, I was a sucker for long, dark lashes, broad shoulders, and bedroom eyes. I looked away, mortified, because I thought my experience with the male species had taught me to look beyond physical attributes and into a place called "personality." And, judging by the way he looked, all self-assured and arrogant, Chase couldn't possibly have much going on for him in the personality department.

"I think this is all a mistake," I said.

I didn't know why I was so angry all of a sudden, but I yanked my hand away a bit too harshly and threw Jude my most venomous look.

"Gotta go. Good luck, you two," Jude said, and before I could protest, she was out the door.

The traitor!

She was the one who had brought this on me. So, obviously, she shouldn't be the one running. Besides, the guy could still be a creep. Or a killer. Or both.

I took a deep breath and let it out slowly as I turned to Chase, almost struck speechless again. But only almost, because I thought I had found the perfect recipe for dealing with those blue eyes and the strange expression in them. I'd either ask him to leave, or I'd deal with him like a professional adult. Seeing that he was already here, I decided to give him a chance.

One opportunity to prove himself. If he blew it, that was it.

"Mr...." I trailed off, waiting for him to fill in the blanks.

"Just Chase." He crossed his arms over his broad chest and regarded me coolly. "Is that what you're wearing?" He raised a brow and pointed at my jacket, the slightest hint of amusement on his lips.

I frowned, perplexed by his sudden straightforwardness. *Jerk with a capital "J."*

"Actually, this is just camouflage for my *real* outfit," I said coolly. "You know, the one I'm hiding underneath it." I fought the urge to roll my eyes. Seriously, why were people ganging up against my outfit? Was it really that bad? I raised my chin defiantly and narrowed my eyes on him, challenging him. "Why? You don't like it?"

"I do. I'm just used to women wearing"—he paused, and his mouth twitched at the corners—"let's just say, other kinds of clothes whenever they have a date with me."

*I bet.*

"This isn't a date. It's a job interview," I muttered, and grabbed my handbag, heading out the door in the hope that he'd follow. He chuckled behind me, and I called over my shoulder, "*I'm* interviewing *you*," just in case his mighty ego might have misinterpreted the situation.

With guys like him, you never knew.

Actually, with guys like him, you needed to spell out that they weren't the only male specimens in the world. "Just so you know, I have a date after this meeting"—I made sure to emphasize the word—"so we'd better hurry."

"Great. Let's get this over with." In spite of his choice of words, he actually sounded excited.

I clamped my mouth shut and let him take the lead.

Chase's car was parked outside, and, to my surprise, it was the sort of sleek sports thingy you'd usually see on television, racing or involved in a road accident.

"Here you go." He opened the door, and I stopped to stare. For a low-paid actor, he seemed to be able to afford an expensive car. Even the doors didn't open sideways, but upward, which was unnatural. But kind of cool. The thought managed to irritate me even more.

Chase held the door open, and I slumped into the black leather seat, marveling at how smooth and cool it felt against my skin. I followed him from the corner of my eyes as he rounded the car and slipped into the driver's seat. Then I asked casually, "Where are we going?"

"It's a surprise." The engine roared to life. The noise was so loud I slumped deeper into my seat before one of the neighbors could see me and think I had joined a gang.

*Chapter 2*

*TAKE A LEAP of faith, Laurie.*

Following Jude's words, I breathed in and out to calm my nerves. Upon my request, Chase had opened the window, and now I was literally swallowing whole chunks of the cold air as it wafted in, in the hope that the wind would infuse some sense of reality into me. It had been such a long time since I'd last gone out with a man that I had forgotten how to make small talk, let alone lead a meaningful conversation. Luckily, Chase knew how to fill the uncomfortable silence that had been looming over my head like a curse ever since our meeting.

"I thought you might like a good, old Texan meal."

"It's fine," I croaked, damning myself for demanding he

open the window in the first place because my throat had turned dry and sore.

"I can still take us somewhere else." Raising his brows, he looked at me sideways, and for a moment our eyes connected in the semi-darkness of the car. My heart took another unwelcome dive.

I shook my head, unable to utter a single word, and interlaced my fingers in my lap, squeezing hard until the skin felt painfully taut.

Wherever he was taking me was okay.

I wasn't planning on staying for dessert anyway. I smiled at myself because I had it all figured out. Get a salad or something while asking him a few questions while pretending that he was a suitable candidate, then fire him. Not on the spot, of course, because, obviously, I didn't want him to be offended, or—worse yet—seek revenge for wasting his time. But fire him nevertheless, after I called a cab home, which would be right after one drink. Until then I would stay friendly. Professional. Endure his boring chats and his obnoxious confidence.

Because, to be realistic, good looks or not, Chase wasn't suitable for the job.

*God, it was such a fantastic plan!*

Jude would be pleased that I had done my best to find a suitable fiancé, and I could go back to brainstorming a less vacuous idea. Duty done, and no hard feelings.

The car took a sharp right, and we drove in silence for another minute or two before Chase asked, "Do you mind if I turn on the music?" Without waiting for my reply, he turned on the radio and closed the window.

Great, he probably thought I was boring. Possibly the worst company he'd ever had. My smile was wiped off my face. I sank deeper into my seat, ready to drown in my mortification.

"So, what's this job all about?" Chase asked, tapping his fingers to some pop charts tune—exactly the kind of music I would have expected him to like. The question didn't exactly take me by surprise. I had thought about my answer and knew exactly what to say.

"I need a fiancé. A future husband."

Only it didn't come out as clever and poised as I had planned. I pushed a stray strand of hair out of my face and turned to catch his reaction. He was smiling—the kind of smile I'd have gladly slapped off his face if I weren't against violence.

"I didn't mean—" I began, then closed my mouth as his gaze turned on me, and heat rushed to my face.

"Usually, I need a proposal first, but I'll make an exception for you."

He was laughing at me.

Damn him!

I cringed as another hot wave of humiliation washed

over me.

"I'm twenty-two, a college graduate, and very much in love with my independence," I said through gritted teeth. "Unfortunately, where I come from, that's not an acceptable status."

I shrugged because that was all I wanted to explain. In fact, I didn't need to explain myself to this stranger at all. The guy would be history by tomorrow anyway, and then he could go back to his manicures and scantily clad women kind of life, while I'd gladly return to my matchbox apartment and boring nights in.

"And I'm twenty-eight, not a college graduate, and very much in love with my independence." He shrugged. "You see, we already have one of three things in common. If that doesn't make for a great pretend engagement, then I don't know what will."

The car pulled abruptly into a dark side road. To either side stretched what looked like warehouses closed for the night. The moon was obscured by dense rain clouds, bathing the area in scary darkness. Apart from a car or two passing us by, nothing stirred. This was absolutely what I had expected—the knowledge hit me like a rock in the pit of my stomach.

*My date was a psycho.*

My gut feeling had been right all along, and Jude sucked—big time. I swallowed hard and gently pushed my hand into my handbag, my fingers fishing for my cell phone, ready to call the police and communicate my whereabouts…as soon as I found out where we were. Or, if there wasn't enough time, I'd fish out the pepper spray I always carried with me.

I craned my neck to look for a street sign, anything to give away my whereabouts, when the tires screeched on the wet asphalt.

Chase pulled into a parking lot and killed the engine. I peered up at the dimly lit building in front of us, and my jaw dropped.

"Is this a—" I almost choked on the word.

"A biker bar?"

*A strip joint,* I wanted to ask, but realized I might have gotten the picture before me all wrong. The blinking lights of a woman standing in front of what looked like a stripping pole were open to interpretation. In fact, I wasn't even sure it was a woman. Maybe a guy with really tall legs leaning against the corner of a building? Or maybe it was supposed to be a very thin slice of bacon wrapped around a fork?

"It used to be a strip club. They haven't changed the sign yet," Chase said, sensing my confusion.

"Exactly your thing, I bet." The words left my mouth before I could stop them. To my surprise, Chase just laughed and opened the door, then walked around the car to help me out.

I grabbed my handbag, pressing it against my chest in case we were mugged, even though, from the look of the dark parking lot, there were only a few parked cars and no people around. It probably wasn't a particularly popular place, I deduced as I watched Chase lock up behind us.

"Initially, I wanted to take you to a nice restaurant, but I figured you might need to loosen up a bit." His eyes bored into mine, and for a moment we just stared at each other. In the moonless night, the ocean-blue color looked like a raging storm.

"That's nice. At least we can share a BBQ plate and get the beer thrown in for free," I muttered. "That is, if we don't get involved in a bar brawl." *Or catch hepatitis,* I added mentally.

I had taken a shaky step forward when his arm wrapped around my waist and he pulled me close, towering over me.

"Relax, Laurie. No one's going to bite you," he said with a glimmer in his eyes. "Unless you ask nicely, in which case, make sure to ask me first."

His hot breath brushed my earlobe, cutting off my air supply and sending an electric frisson of excitement down my spine. From so close, he smelled amazing, of aftershave and something else. Something dark and earthy and way too sexy.

I pressed my handbag harder against my chest, ready to

sling it over my shoulder and put some space between us, but his arm released me, and he stepped aside.

Opening the door to the bar, he motioned for me to enter.

"Ladies first."

I had no idea whether he was laughing at me again, so I nodded a "thank you" and stepped inside the bar.

# Chapter 3

THE BAR WAS a crowded single room with tables on one side and a bar area on the other where the mostly male patrons had gathered in a neat row, nursing their drinks. As suspected, the place looked like it had seen better days, and its clientele seemed past its prime, too. AC/DC was playing at a bearable level in the background. As we walked in, a few heads turned. Bleak eyes slipped over me, barely paying me a second look, which I assumed was the result of my outfit. I didn't mind because I didn't like to stand out in a crowd anyway.

Chase's fingers touched the low of my back and guided me to the bar area. Immediately, two guys with tattoos covering most of their exposed skin stood and offered me a seat. I whispered a thank-you and sat down, slowly relaxing the grip around my handbag.

"This is the last place you probably expected to meet chivalry," Chase remarked, amused, and turned to greet one of the guys who, from the look of it, he seemed to know pretty well.

I sighed inwardly.

Not only was I stuck with a guy who thought it might be a good idea to have a job interview in his regular bar, he also seemed to have forgotten all about me while touching base with his buddy.

Crossing my legs, I ignored them as my attention focused on the bar area and the man serving drinks behind it. He was maybe in his early thirties, clad in jeans and a black T-shirt featuring the logo of a band that had seen better days—both the band and the T-shirt. His eyes met mine and his face lit up, his dark eyes glittering with something.

I smiled shyly.

Now, *he* seemed like a better candidate.

*Candidate.*

I really liked that word. It almost made me feel like Donald Trump on *The Apprentice*. Right now I would have loved to point my finger at Chase while saying, "You're fired."

"Drink?" The bartender pushed a bottle of beer over the

counter before I could declare my distaste for anything alcoholic. It wasn't that I didn't like the taste of it; I just didn't like what alcohol did to me. I smiled again and took a customary sip. "Not your usual place, huh?"

I nodded. "I guess you could say that."

He wiped his hand on a towel and held it out. "I'm Adam."

"Laurie." I gave his hand a quick squeeze and pulled back quickly.

"Great to meet you, Laurie," he said. I laughed because, for some reason, his open smile was infectious. "I'm sure Chase will show you the ropes."

Following Adam's line of vision, I turned and found Chase behind me, watching me with a strange look. Suddenly uncomfortable, I took another sip of my beer, even though I had already overstepped my personal limit, and followed his movements as he grabbed a bottle from Adam, then pointed to the back of the room.

"There's a free table over there. Given the purpose of this meeting, I thought you might welcome the privacy." Chase shrugged, as though it was a mere suggestion, but his fingers wrapped around my elbow decisively. I had no doubt if I didn't get up, he'd help me to my feet—possibly by dragging me up. I remained seated.

"Privacy?" Adam laughed, and Chase narrowed his eyes at him.

"Mind your damn business, Adam."

There was a sharp undertone to his voice, a hard edge I hadn't detected before. I looked up but saw nothing reflected in Chase's face. Adam flashed me a smile and turned away, mumbling something like, "If you need anything..."

"Come on," Chase murmured in my ear, sending a strange jolt through my stomach. We zigzagged our way through the room to a table on the far side near the tinted windows, and Chase held out my chair, his attention strangely distracted as he sat down in his own chair, his relaxed attitude suddenly replaced by tension.

"You two know each other," I remarked as a means of starting the conversation.

"Yeah." He smirked and shifted in his seat, then pointed around him. "Like it?" I knew an attempt to change topics when I saw one, even one as smooth as Chase's.

I decided to let it pass this time. For one, it wasn't my business. Besides, it didn't matter, considering I'd be leaving soon anyway and would never see him again. "It's—" I fought to find the right word as I scanned the exotic bottles adorning the walls and the peanut shells littering the hardwood floor.

"Interesting," I said eventually. "Never seen a place like this from the inside. Is this the sort of establishment you usually frequent?"

"You make it sound like it's a strip bar." His stunning blue eyes twinkled and his lips twitched with amusement, striking me breathless once again. The Chase from before was back, and hotter, if that was even possible.

"Given that you *knew* this used to be a strip bar and probably used to frequent it, you can't judge me for forming such a first impression."

"Touché."

We fell silent for a few moments, listening to the song changing in the background—something lighter, more my style. I began to tap my fingers on my thigh, nervous under Chase's blue gaze.

There we were, and I had no clue how to get it over and done with. I figured being tactful was the way to go.

But how?

"This job," Chase began slowly, "it's not something I've ever done before. I just thought you should know."

Not surprising, given the fact that most people I knew either weren't single or weren't afraid of admitting it to their family. They sure as hell didn't need a paid actor to play the doting fiancé part, and they certainly didn't need to pretend to be in love and ready to walk down the aisle.

"That's fine. I didn't expect you to, because I know my situation is bizarre."

*And desperate.*

He shook his head and leaned forward, placing his hand

on the table so close his fingers almost brushed mine.

"It's not the most bizarre request I've ever had. Trust me on that." His eyes twinkled, and for a second I wasn't sure whether he was being serious or teasing me. "Once, I was asked to play a monkey on stage. If I can imitate an orangutan, I'm pretty sure I can play your husband."

I stared at him. He was trying to be funny. And it worked. Too easily. Only too late did I realize I had been smiling without even wanting to.

"Fiancé," I corrected.

"Even better. We can play the loved-up couple without all the insults and the hating that comes with being married."

I laughed. "Not a fan of the so-called wedding bliss?"

"You could say that." He smirked before a sexy smile lit up his lips again. "What about you?"

I shrugged as I thought back to my old life and began to flick through what I could and couldn't say. In the end, I decided some things were better left unsaid. "It doesn't really matter."

"Why do you need a fake fiancé?" Chase asked, proving to be a guru at changing the subject. "Can't you just say you're not into it?" His directness took me again by surprise. "Surely if you don't live with your parents anymore, which I think you're not"—he paused, his expression questioning. I nodded and he continued—" then you don't owe them an explanation."

I brushed my hair back, hesitating. Explaining my situation without actually explaining anything was the hard part. Jude was the only person who knew my dilemma. She was the only person who knew some of the secrets that surrounded Waterfront Shore.

I needed it to stay that way.

"I can't deal with it right now," I said simply. It was the truth, to some extent. "I know I sound like a coward, but there's enough drama in my life already. All I want is to buy myself a little bit more time." I gave an uncomfortable shrug.

"No, you're not a coward." He shook his head slowly, his eyes piercing through my heart and soul—so deep my breath caught in my throat. Even though I knew he was trying to be polite, somehow it mattered that Chase didn't think of me that way.

I leaned back, eyeing him more carefully.

Perhaps Jude was right, and Chase was a nice guy.

"I think it's unselfish," he continued. "Maybe you're holding on to the hope that one day you'll find the one person who'll change your outlook. And when you do, maybe someday you'll give your parents what they want."

I highly doubted that, so I inclined my head and forced my lips into a thin smile. He couldn't have the entire situation more wrong. Love and marriage had never been one of my priorities. They had never featured in my cards because love is nothing but a fool's gold: It glitters and shines until you look underneath and see that all is but an empty shell of appearance. Something we all want but can never fully grasp, and when we do, it always comes with heartbreak.

I stopped wanting love a long time ago.

"Maybe," I lied, ready to change the subject. "Your Internet profile says that you're an actor. You certainly look the part." My face flushed a little at the obvious compliment.

Chase's smile widened. He'd opened his mouth to say something when I held up my hand, stopping him before he got the wrong idea and thought I was hitting on him, which I wasn't…not intentionally, anyway.

"What I mean is, you don't look like you need to do this kind of job to get by." Damn, that came out wrong, too. I cringed. "What I mean is—"

"I get it," Chase said, laughing. "Acting doesn't pay a lot. In our economy, you have to get creative. I do a bit of theater acting, host workshops for aspiring models and TV personalities, do club appearances, voice-overs. You know, bits and pieces here and there." He paused for a moment and took a gulp of his drink, obviously in his element. "I draw the line at nude work. In fact, at anything involving nudity."

My fantasy took off in that instant, and I found myself imagining him half-naked. His body looked buff enough to earn him a lot of money. Actors certainly didn't wear a whole lot of clothes—particularly not those who looked like Chase—so why not go just a little bit further than that? Everyone did it. Not that I wanted him to.

The mere thought of him strolling in front of a camera with his shirt off ignited a pang of fire inside me.

"I get it," I lied. *Not.* With a body as hot as his, shoulders that broad and arms that strong, it should have been mandatory for him to show off his sexiness.

Chase took a gulp of his beer and put the bottle back down, the clear liquid leaving a wet trail on his full lips. Unintentionally, I brushed a trembling hand through my curls. I wasn't used to sitting so close to someone, especially someone so manly and confident. I had never met anyone who had made my body react the way it did around Chase.

I averted my gaze quickly before he noticed and leaned back, taking a sharp breath and letting it out slowly.

Okay, I didn't really know him after barely spending an hour in his presence, but so far he had been friendly and easygoing, nonjudgmental and way more fun than I imagined. Chase had proved that he wasn't what I expected at all, and, to my surprise, I found that I actually enjoyed his company. Only a few days left until I had to face the Waterfront Shore dilemma. Only a few days to come up with a better plan.

If only I knew how to get out of my problems. I had been searching for months, and there was no better plan. None that might actually work.

Except hiring an actor.

"How good is your acting?" I found myself asking, my hands playing with the neck of the beer bottle.

"I would say 'good.' If we're to work together, then I'll obviously need to get into character," Chase said before I could follow the strange direction of my thoughts. "Find out everything about you. Who you really are. What you do. What makes you tick. You know the drill."

I turned to regard Chase's smooth face and the smile lighting up his eyes.

He wanted to know me to get into character. A dangerous undertaking, but not impossible. A challenge on my part to give him what he wanted while not giving him anything at all. It might just be simple enough.

*Not a good idea. Back off, Hanson.*

Alarm bells went off somewhere in my mind as I found myself nodding slowly.

"We'll have to agree on a fee," I said in spite of my better judgment.

"I'm affordable. You can even pay in installments." His lips twitched at the corners as he reached over the table and held out his hand, urging me to shake it. "Do we have a deal?"

The words came low, insinuating hidden promises and dark secrets, and my heart lurched in my chest. "You haven't even asked what exactly this role entails. For all you know, I could be asking impossible things of you. Like…" I threw my hands up in exasperation as my words failed me.

"I'm strong enough to fend off any unwanted advances," Chase said. "I'm cool if you want me to be." Something in his tone made me turn back to him. His facial expression was serious now; even the glint of amusement in his eyes had disappeared.

"There won't be any sort of advances," I said sharply.

"My life philosophy is 'deal with whatever's thrown your way when the time comes,' Laurie." The way he said my name sent a tiny shiver down my spine.

Sexy.

Forbidden.

As if he knew me already. Too personal for my taste.

I gawked at him, both confused and irritated by my strong reaction to something as basic as the way he pronounced my name. It wasn't like me to be so—

*Animalistic?*

That's what sex is all about, isn't it? An instinct. A pull that isn't reasonable or easily understood. I hadn't been with someone like him in a long time. Rewind that. I had never been with someone like him. Someone who exuded sexuality in such an obvious yet non-intrusive way.

The fact I had never experienced what sex felt like, and then sitting opposite what I assumed might be the world's sexiest man alive, was painful in both a physical and mental sense. I was craving what shouldn't be craved, seeking what I should have run from.

Chase rolled up his sleeves, exposing strong arms, and leaned forward. My heart rate spiked and my body temperature began to rise—the result of a lack of air conditioning, I assumed. Or maybe it was because my mind kept creating images of him in bed, and I kept wondering if his kisses would be as delicious as he looked.

As if sensing my thoughts, Chase leaned back in his chair, and his gaze settled on my mouth for a second or two. My lips parted of their own accord, as though inviting him to savor them, even though that was the last thing I wanted. He raised his eyebrows, and his lips slowly curled into a sexy smile. And there it was again—a spark of something way too intimate as our eyes met.

"Do you believe in destiny, Laurie?" His voice was deep and dark, the strange tone drawing my attention back to him instantly.

"No. I just believe in reality." I swallowed hard. "If it's destiny, then it's a heck of a cruel life. Never to be able to guess what happens next, always having to find a meaning. I want to make a choice, not be thrown in it." I paused and looked up. He was watching me intently, his expression unreadable. "Do you?"

"I think it takes two to meet true destiny and two to hold on to it. To me, it's not a matter of a superpower at play, but more a higher awareness of what you need and can achieve when it comes to what you want. True destiny is a complex interplay of two people playing and working together," he said. "I can help you, Laurie. You just need to ask if you want to work with me."

His hand touched mine, scorching my skin. I took a sharp breath, my gaze instantly drawn to our hands. But before I could withdraw from his touch, he pulled away.

Chase's willingness to come close, to touch and probably be touched, screamed that he was open for more. But he wasn't pushy about it.

*You need to get laid.*

Jude's voice kept echoing in my head. If it hadn't been for her calling Chase to arrange this meeting, I would never have been in such a situation.

Damn her and her idiotic plans.

Damn her for finding the one specimen who was too sexy to ignore.

My hands began to tremble just a little bit. I interlaced my fingers the way I always did when I needed to stop them from shaking, and inclined my head.

Was it a wise move to go through with this? Probably

not. But I was a grown-up woman who had her emotions and bodily urges under control. Whatever was going on today was an exception. Maybe the result of stress or nerves, but certainly nothing to worry about.

"We'll give it a trial run," I found myself saying. "Let's see how the evening goes, and then we'll take it from there."

"No." He shook his head, his lips twitching. "You need to make a decision now. It's either you take me or not. So, Laurie." My heart stopped in its tracks as he pushed his chair back and went down on one knee, grabbing my hand in the process. "Will you give me the honor and be my fake wife?"

I stared at him, struck speechless. He made it sound so simple. Uncomplicated. No further questions. Exactly what I needed for my plan to work. Maybe I was overthinking things.

"Hell, let's do it." I grinned at him and shook his hand. As I turned around, I saw people staring. I could only guess it wasn't usual for a newly engaged couple to shake hands rather than fall into each other's arms. Not exactly a romantic moment. Nothing to gush about. Not even a ring.

But, for some reason, it felt perfect nonetheless.

"Great. Let's order," Chase said, and patted the chair next to him. "I'm starving. One of the first things you should know about your future husband is that I'm always hungry." The glint in his eyes appeared again, and for the first time I realized it wasn't just amusement. He was testing me to see if I'd withdraw my offer and back off.

I bit my lip hard, wondering whether I was making a mistake.

*No going back on your word, Hanson. You're working with him. It's just a business deal, not a real relationship, and certainly no falling in love.*

Damn right I wasn't going to back off. Because, in spite of what people thought, I wasn't a coward. I wasn't a helpless romantic.

I was a fighter.

And Chase would help me win my own fight.

Chapter 4

"READY TO SEE your fiancé?" Jude's head popped in around the door. Her voice pricked my bubble filled with hope of getting any work done.

"Please don't tell me Chase is already here."

"He's just arrived." She shot me her most saccharine smile. "If you want, I can keep him busy."

"No, it's all right." I sighed at her smitten smile and got up from my bed, shutting my laptop in the process. Ever since I'd told her about my decision to let Chase play the part, she couldn't stop referring to him as my "fiancé." And how lucky I was to have found this "hottie." Never mind the fact that I only knew his last name—Wright—and a few tidbits about his life. Like the fact that he was twenty-eight years old, a part-time actor who grew up in the hot South and would rather spend his days riding through the wooded pastures than lounging by a pool. Jude was convinced that everything else was just décor, as in—

First, the character...not important. In her words, "The guy's hot. Who could possibly want to focus on a meaningful conversation in his presence anyway when his body could do all the talking?"

Second, the past...let's be honest, who doesn't have a closet full of secrets and probably a few skeletons?

Third, bad habits...in his case, easily overlooked because...see point one.

In short, Chase had to be good because he was sexy. Talk about being objectifying, which she was, even though I would never have called her out on it.

After all of ten minutes speaking with him on the phone and a few more minutes of seeing him in real life, Jude was in lust, hook, line, and sinker. And now she was literally begging me to dig my fingers into him, or give her my sloppy seconds so she could find out if an actor not only looked but also played the part.

While I laughed at her outrageous suggestion, a jolt of unease hit me yet again, only this time, as I slipped into my jacket, I pondered what it could possibly mean.

Chase was a good-looking guy, charming and groomed. We had gotten on well the previous night. Maybe even too well because, right after our short dinner, he had brought me straight home, as if our arrangement had settled everything and there was nothing else to discuss.

Granted, his easygoing attitude and the fact that he wasn't taking himself too seriously had been a relief. Much to my surprise, we even shared my life philosophy on commitment: We both didn't like the idea of being tied down. And, just like me, he was focused on work and success. So I knew there would be no invisible questionnaires to assess a prospective life partner and his outlook on the future, no mentally planning the wedding and choosing the kids' name.

I attributed my sudden uneasy streak to the fact that he was the only candidate I had for now, and consequently, in a twisted kind of way, I was being over-possessive and overly cautious, not wanting to make a mistake that would overcomplicate things, such as sleeping with the "help."

Count in the fact that he was about to help me out big time, and he was all mine—on a strictly platonic level. Which was why I had insisted on meeting with him in the afternoon, just for coffee, to set up some rules that would keep any blurred lines clear and would ensure our business deal couldn't possibly steer into a sexual attraction direction, which meant:

No gazing into each other's eyes in a dimly lit room.

No *accidentally* touching each other's hands while

reaching for a drink.

And certainly no awkward moment of parting ways while standing in the doorway and pondering the idea of inviting him in just to see what happens—like the one brainless moment I'd had the day before when I wondered whether he was as toned as he looked.

"I have yet to come up with a better solution, so, in some way, I depend on this guy," I said. "Promise you won't embarrass me, Jude."

"What? Me?" Her eyes widened with false innocence. I *knew* that look. The conniving little witch!

"Jude!" I hissed, peering toward the door to make sure Chase wasn't there. "I mean it. No hints or remarks. No sexual innuendos. And definitely no help to get him to *like* me." Which was something she always did by telling guys "cute" little stories about me, reminiscent of a mother doting over her child. Needless to say, it always backfired.

"You mean like *like* you." She grinned. "Or—"

"You know exactly what I mean," I hissed, cutting her short. "Keep your mouth shut at all times, please."

She shrugged. "Whatever. If you want to stick to your boring life, I'll accept your decision."

I could see from the stubborn look on her face that she harbored no intention of keeping her word, but I had no time to argue. Throwing her a warning look, I grabbed my handbag and walked past her.

"You look stunning," Chase said with an appreciative smile as I entered the living room.

"You think?" I made a clumsy pirouette and regarded him coolly. "You don't look so bad yourself."

He was dressed in jeans and yet another snug shirt that accentuated his chiseled chest. His dark hair was tousled in an effortless way, and the onset of a stubble cast shadows on his chin and cheeks, giving his gray-blue gaze a haunted look. My heart jerked against my ribcage and sank into my jeans as I regarded him in silence. He wasn't just delicious; he made me wonder what secrets lay hidden beyond those eyes.

"Ready to kick back?" Chase asked.

"Hell, yeah, she is," Jude said with a wink at me. She had insisted on canceling her afternoon date to see me off, as in, spend some time around Chase in case I might pass him on to her. "That's all we've been talking about all day," she continued.

*Oh, here we go.*

For the umpteenth time I felt like strangling her. That was all *she* had been talking about while I had been trying to focus on work, as in skimming various newspapers and an entire bookmarks section on my laptop for various employment opportunities. As usual, my attempts had remained fruitless. No one wanted to employ an out-of-college graduate with no hands-on work experience and no references. Never mind the fact that I had tried to obtain all of the above during my time at college, only to be fobbed off with the excuse that a college degree was a prerequisite for actually getting any sort of work experience.

"Is that so? You've been talking about me?" Chase said, interrupting my thoughts.

"Not really." I smirked and realized from his smug expression that he didn't believe a word. The problem with guys like him was that, not only were their looks too perfect for their own good, but their ego usually matched the proportion of their looks. "Jude is being far too generous." I eyed her behind his back, mouthing, *Shut up*.

We said goodbye to Jude, who even accompanied us to the door and pulled us in a hug in a bold moment of lust-induced craziness. I grimaced at her because she had never been the hugging type. In fact, she always claimed touching other people's skin gave her the itches.

And then we were in Chase's car, finally alone. He pulled out of the quiet residential area and onto the busy highway, out of the city.

"Are we going back to your favorite bar?" I asked casually.

He looked at me sideways and smiled. "That was my first choice, but I figured it's probably closed until dusk because of all the honest people who could accidentally find their way over there. We wouldn't want that."

"Ah. A bar that chooses its clientele wisely. Makes sense." I nodded knowingly. "What makes you think only crooks should visit the place?"

"You did yesterday," Chase said. I raised my brows, and he continued, "You kept your handbag glued to your chest like it was a life preserver."

"I thought I was going to get mugged," I muttered. "You can't blame me for being too careful."

His lips quirked, and for a heartbeat I felt compelled to reach over and touch his cheek just to see whether his stubble would graze my skin as deliciously as I imagined it would.

"I'm taking you to a special place," Chase said, oblivious to the naughty direction of my thoughts. "You'll like it. It should be more...your style."

I narrowed my eyes. "And what do you think my style is?"

"Interesting." He looked at me, ignoring my puzzled expression. "Just wait."

We made small talk for a few minutes, talking mostly about my day's events, or lack thereof, and then he left the highway and pulled onto unpaved terrain. Gravel creaked under the tires as we passed a gate marking the land beyond as private property. The narrow road stretched on for a mile or two, after which Chase parked the car and we exited.

"Where are we?" I asked, turning slowly to take in the

area. To either side were hills of grapevines and untouched nature. Even the air smelled clean and fresh.

"You'll see," he said mysteriously.

## Chapter 5

THE SUN SHIMMERED in the sky, its bright rays warming my skin. I took off my jacket, revealing a loose batwing top, and slung it over my arm as I followed Chase along a narrow path up a hill. Gravel and loose branches crunched under my heels. Once or twice, Chase supported my arm to prevent me from taking a tumble. As we reached the top, I saw the meadow below. Almost hidden between orange trees was a picturesque cottage with whitewashed walls and painted windowsills.

I stopped to draw a sharp breath, not because it was so amazingly beautiful, but because it reminded me of Waterfront Shore...of the oleander bushes growing all over the property, shading us from the blazing midday sun.

"Come on. We're nearly there." With a silent smile, Chase grabbed my hand and pulled me after him. He didn't let go until we reached the porch. A table and two chairs had already been set up, a white tablecloth covering the old wood, giving it an old but charming flair. The cottage was run-down in some way, and yet it made me feel more at home than any other place ever had. Maybe it was because it was planted in the middle of nature, a direct contrast to the city I lived in.

A soft wind pushed a strand of hair into my face, and eventually I turned my head away from the stunning scene and back toward him. "I hope we're not trespassing," I said.

He shook his head, his gray-blue eyes shadowed by those impossibly dark lashes that kept me mesmerized. "No, it's mine."

"Really?" I asked, surprised.

"I bought it a while ago. It was supposed to be an investment. Then I realized living in the city might be good for your pocket, but nature's good for the soul. I need to switch off whenever the chance presents itself, so I come down here on the weekends. Sometimes even during the week."

He pulled a chair back and gestured for me to sit. I sat down and peered at Chase, unsure what to say. When he had claimed to want to show me a special place, I figured he was talking about something more public. To be honest, I didn't expect any of it. Not the complete solitude. Nor the privacy, or the stunning views.

"I'll get us something to drink. Chilled white wine good for you?" Chase asked.

"Yes. Thank you," I said, and leaned back in my chair, inhaling the aroma of oranges as I closed my eyes for a few seconds, savoring the way the sun warmed my skin. I only opened them at the sound of approaching footsteps and took a glass of wine out of Chase's hand.

"It's beautiful here," I began, pointing my glass to the stunning hills surrounding the cottage. "And so serene."

"Yeah." He smiled. "It's the closest I could get to my home. Did I tell you where I grew up?"

"Texas," I said.

He nodded. "I was born in Mulberry and spent the first few years of my life there." His eyes clouded over, but only for a moment, during which he didn't reply. "My parents used to travel a lot, meaning I've lived all over the world."

"But your accent—"

He cut me off. "It's an acquired thing. My father was born in Kerr, so that's where I grew up. But my grandparents used to live near Lake Superior in Michigan. I used to stay with them every now and then when my parents were on tour, doing their thing. They were performers with a huge entourage." He took a sip of his wine. In the bright sun, he looked more stunning than ever.

For the first time, I noticed the golden glow of his skin and the beautiful contrast it built to his gray-blue eyes. I figured he spent a lot of time outside in the sun.

"It must have been quite exciting to travel so much," I said.

"It was okay, I guess." He shrugged. "Taking care of a child at home when you'd rather hang out with famous people and party until the clubs throw you out was quite the pain in the ass for my parents and not exactly what I'd call a normal childhood. When I was young, I used to envy people who had a stable home rather than live in a bus. As I got older, I got increasingly bored with the routine and looked forward to our brief periods at home. Luckily, my grandparents were happy to give me a shot at that. They took good care of me." I ignored the sudden leap my heart took, because it was the longest Chase had ever talked about himself. I barely knew anything about him, so the insight into his past fascinated me.

"During the summers, we used to visit Muskegon State Park all the time." He looked up, his eyes boring into mine. "Maybe one day we'll go together."

My breath hitched in my throat.

Men said things like that all the time without actually meaning them.

*Empty promises.*

They all made them. They all broke them. I decided

whatever he suggested was just a means of being friendly. In no way was he being serious.

I stated the obvious. "You loved Michigan so much you decided to get rid of your accent."

If Chase noticed my feeble attempt at changing the subject, he let it slide.

"I tried—it sort of stuck with me. But enough about me," he said, his eyes locking on mine. "Tell me something about you, Laurie. How did you get to be this…." He eyed me up and down, lingering on my chest a beat too long, leaving the rest open to interpretation.

I narrowed my eyes. "What?"

"I wanted to say exquisite." He smiled. "But…I'm going with gorgeous?"

*Holy cow.*

I forced my dropped jaw to close.

Maybe he was just being friendly, or maybe he was trying to flirt with me. Whatever it was, his charm was working.

Under his penetrating scrutiny, I flamed up, and my hand traveled up to my chest instinctively. Not to cover up, but to hide the telltale signs of my attraction to him.

Yes, he said some nice things. But it wasn't his words that made my thoughts turn in a direction I didn't want them to take.

It was the way he looked at me…all intense and

broody…with a depth that went beyond mere politeness and casual friendship, way beyond professional relationships and our unwritten contract. The way he regarded me, it was almost as though his eyes couldn't take in enough of me. They settled on my lips too long, and I suppressed the urge to moisten them. No one had ever made me feel so confused—both wanting to dive into his eyes and run away at the same time.

It was exactly the kind of thing I had always wanted to avoid, the reason why I was single, never letting anyone too close. Chase was right on the brink of destroying it by crushing all formalities to dust.

"There's not much to say," I began carefully, and took a sip of the cold wine. His brows drew together, as if he believed I was being modest, and I didn't like it. I had a penchant for staying in the background and not drawing unnecessary attention to myself, but it sure wasn't out of modesty.

"You said you grew up in California. It's a big state," he prompted.

"That's true."

"Where exactly?" His eyes narrowed, and I realized that, for a man, he was extremely observant.

I took a deep breath to bide for time as I pondered my possible answers. How much could I tell him? On the one hand, I didn't want to offend him, or make him suspicious.

On the other, revealing my true past would be too much. In the end, he'd find out anyway, so why not be candid up front, at least about a few things? As my fake fiancé, he had a right to know.

"I grew up on a ranch in Malibu," I began. "Waterfront Shore. It's only a few hours' drive from here. I haven't visited it in years."

"Why?" He leaned forward, genuinely interested.

I shrugged. "Because it's not the kind of life I want to live. I need more than—" I paused again, hesitating. *Money, I wanted to add. Luxury—all the things I gave up for priceless freedom.* It was a slippery slope and a fine line I wasn't yet ready to cross. Chase was getting dangerously close to me, and I wasn't prepared to reveal too much.

"Just more," I said, and smiled. "Even as a child, I was bored out of my mind, so I decided to travel. Get an education. Do something with my life. I applied for college, packed my bags, and did the one thing I had been dreaming of doing ever I since I felt the need to be free."

"Leave."

"Yeah. Leave my parents' home."

"Just like me," he said softly.

"Yeah." I looked at him bitterly, ignoring the sudden feeling that he was trying to see inside me. The *inner* me. The part that was too ugly to ever be exposed. If only he knew why I had to leave. Why my life at home had ended for good. Why I had been in shambles for many years, unable to mend what was left of my past. "The moment I turned eighteen, it was like my path had been written in stone for me. No going back, now or ever."

He cocked his head to the side, his gaze intense again. "A relationship gone bad?"

It was a simple question, and yet I couldn't stop the shudder running down my spine. Shaking my head, I took a deep breath as I tried to push the dark thoughts to the back of my mind before they grabbed hold of me, keeping me hostage in their clutches. "It wasn't because of a guy. I have never been much the dating kind, you know."

What drove me away hadn't been a lover. No relationship or unrequited love. It had been much deeper than that. Much closer to my heart, and consequently much more painful. Dangerous. Precarious. Every step of my path had been carefully planned—the results of endless weighing up sides and taking no risks.

"What made you leave?" I asked.

"The same as you," Chase said. "I knew there was a world out there. I had glimpsed it through the windows of my parents' tour bus, and I wanted a piece of it. I felt a need to do something unexpected and maybe even find my own place in life along the way."

"So, no dirty secret?" I teased.

"I'm afraid not," he said seriously.

"You wanted to find yourself, then."

"And define myself." He nodded, deep in thought. "My parents never taught me who I was. It was life that showed me that. It helped me find what I needed."

For the second time something passed between us. I could feel it in the air. Hear it in the soft chirping of insects. Smell it in the breeze carrying the scent of ripe oranges and something else. *Chase*. His cologne intermingled with the warmth emanating from him.

I gulped down a mouthful of oxygen, and suddenly the air was too thick, choking me, bringing me to a point where my head felt dizzy and the cave of my mouth was too parched to speak.

"I've got to go," I croaked, and had risen to my feet when my feet gave away beneath me. My fingers wrapped around the back of the chair for support, but Chase was faster. One arm wrapped around my waist and he pulled me against him, making the dizzy spell worse.

"Whoa. Sit down." His deep voice sent a pulsating shiver through me as he moved the chairs and the table away from the sun and then helped me back into my seat. "It's the damn heat. It would knock everyone down."

"I'm okay," I whispered, and even managed a half-smile, which was meant to infuse enough confidence in him that he'd let me go, even though every part of my body longed to be touched. Away from the merciless sun, I started to feel better.

"Can I get you some cold water?" Chase asked, brushing my hair away from my sweat-covered face. I grimaced, realizing it probably wasn't a pretty sight.

"No. I'll be fine. But thanks."

"You sure?" He sounded doubtful. His brows drew together as he lifted my chin to meet his worried gaze.

"Did you actually eat anything today?"

I shook my head, barely able to breathe with him so close. Our lips were inches away—a distance easily closed in a heartbeat. My pulse picked up in speed as I fought the urge to press my mouth against his just to see whether he tasted as good as he smelled.

"I'll make you something."

Before I could protest, Chase's hand had released me, and I found myself sitting in the chair, staring after him as he entered the house, leaving the door ajar. That was when I realized he hadn't invited me in.

I didn't mean to be prying, but, for some unknown reason, I felt a strong need to discover more about him, about the way he lived, who he was. Craning my neck, I scanned the narrow hall. Apart from two framed pictures on the walls and a rain jacket hanging from a hook, it was empty.

I shielded my eyes against the sun to get a better glimpse of the pictures and realized one of them was of a gate leading up to a beautiful backyard. The rich green foliage and flowers in various colors built a strong contrast to the thin fog that gave the entire setting a haunted allure. The second picture showed a man standing near a sea and holding a big fish from a hook, his facial expression reflecting his pride.

At the sound of approaching footsteps, I turned my head, my eyes focused on the blooming orange trees.

From the corner of my eye, I watched him put down a large bamboo plate with fresh bread and cheese, red grapes, and freshly sliced watermelon. To my dismay, he pulled his chair to mine and sat down so close our thighs touched. I regarded him as he began to pile cheese on a thin slice of bread, silently urging me to take a bite.

The air around us thickened again with tension and anticipation. This kind of closeness was exactly what I had tried to avoid. Away from civilization, his gesture, coupled with sitting so close to him and sharing the same plate, felt awfully intimate, and even more so when he watched me take a bite. Aware of his intense gaze, my throat constricted, and I forced myself to swallow slowly so I wouldn't choke.

I shifted in my seat, prying my leg off his in the process. If he noticed, he didn't say anything. Instead, he took a bite of his bread and popped a grape into his mouth, signaling me to do the same. I held up my hand and shook my head, smiling weakly as I tried hard to control my breathing. My stomach growled. I knew it was hunger, and something else.

Longing.

Deep-rooted desire.

God, did he *have* to be so stunning? So sinfully sexy it physically hurt me in places I didn't want to acknowledge.

"You need to eat, Laurie."

If only I could.

I lifted a slice of watermelon to my mouth and gingerly took a bite. A few drops of sweet juice gathered on my lips and traveled down my chin. I turned to look at Chase and realized he was staring at me, his eyes dark and hooded. Ever so slowly, his thumb brushed the moisture off my chin, touching my lips in the process.

My breath hitched in my throat. My lips parted, begging him to stop being so nice—so sexy—and just taste them. My body pleaded with him to make a move and kiss me, touch me, and draw me to him so I could finally find out if his lips were as soft as they looked.

"This has to stop," I said, and looked away, regretting my words almost instantly.

Silence ensued.

The seconds seemed to stretch on forever. Eventually, I turned my head back to him and realized he was regarding me, amused.

"There's a reason why I wanted to see you today, Chase." I cringed at the way I pronounced his name—too breathy, too intimate. I had made a promise never to speak it out loud in his presence because he was getting into my head. To my utter humiliation, I realized I hadn't been able to stay resolute for longer than a few minutes. Or maybe it was the effect of the wine, and I wasn't to blame.

Anyway, this came out all wrong. It made me look desperate. And I wasn't that desperate—yet. I tried to force air into my lungs, but my breathing came out all hard and heavy.

"Are you okay?" Chase asked, all fake innocence and concern.

I nodded but didn't dare look at him, afraid of what he might see in my face. Afraid that my inability to control my body's reactions around him would give me away, and he'd realize just how turned on I was by him.

"We need to establish a few rules in our arrangement to stop this from turning into something that can't ever happen," I whispered, finally plucking up the courage to look at him.

He raised his eyebrows as he cocked his head. "What rules?" He sounded so genuine that he almost had me fooled, were it not for the glint in his eyes.

"Good that you're asking. I've made a list." I pulled out a crumpled sheet of paper from my handbag and handed it to him. I peered over his shoulder as his eyes scanned my handwriting, and almost cringed at my choice of words.

No kissing…

No touching…

No invitations to secluded places after midnight, and that involves bedrooms.

"I sound like a deranged lunatic, don't I?" I whispered, my face red with shame.

"It's fine." He folded the paper and handed it back to me. "If that's what you want, I'm okay with it." His gaze scanned my flaming cheeks for a moment. "I'm not like other men. I don't want to do anything that could hurt you, Laurie."

My heart skipped a beat as I realized that he thought my reluctance to play along stemmed from a broken heart and disappointed relationships.

"That's not it," I murmured. "I just want nothing to interfere with the job." Even in my own ears, my voice sounded unconvinced. Shaking. Tumultuous.

For a few long moments, we just stared at each other in silence, the air between us thick like winter's fog. I knew if I dared walk in, I might get lost forever.

A hot wind blew a strand of hair into my face, and I brushed it away. My stomach gave another loud rumble. I took a few bites of food before Chase returned with a glass of water.

"This tastes really good." I pointed to the plate on the table and took the glass from his outstretched hand.

"Did you get a chance to compile the list I asked for so that I know what to answer if people ask questions?" he asked.

I shook my head. "I'll email it to you tomorrow."

"Good." He inclined his head toward the food, again urging me to eat. I followed his silent command, and slowly the air between us cleared and we returned to safer terrain, the conversation flowing easily.

"While my stepfather's in town, I'll need you for a few days. A week tops," I explained. "He'll want to know everything about you. I say we keep to the truth, just bending a few details here and there for the sake of not getting confused." Chase nodded, and I continued. "We don't live together because you travel a lot and need your space. Besides, we don't believe in sex before marriage."

He raised his brows at that, and I stifled a giggle. Obviously, he wasn't on board with that one.

"My family has always been old-fashioned," I explained, even though that didn't exactly apply to the way my stepfather lived his life. "No need to face them with the realities of life."

"Agreed." His lips curled into a stunning, sexy smile that sent my pulse racing faster than a racehorse sprinting. "When are we going to do the deed?"

*Holy shit.*

Talk about double meanings!

The image of him on top of me entered my head, his strong arms pinning me down, our bodies moving in accord while wave after amazing wave of ecstasy rocked my abdomen. The mere image had me so worked up I gasped, suddenly unable to breathe. As if sensing my naughty imagination, Chase's gaze settled on me with an intense expression, and all heat drained from my face.

"What?" His mouth twitched at my shocked reaction. "I need to know in case they ask."

"Obviously, never, because we're not getting married." I smirked. "And they won't ask because sex isn't something we usually discuss. They're old-fashioned when it comes to me. You know, no public displays of affection and all that. Sleeping in separate rooms. The usual." I waved my hand.

"Got it." He nodded again. Underneath his tone I could detect amusement. He was laughing at me, and I couldn't blame him. "Where did we meet?"

That was a tough one. Where do you usually meet a stunning male actor when your family expects you to be a nun with no social life, no interest in the opposite sex, and definitely no flirting skills? Worse yet, how do you keep a handsome guy hooked for months with absolutely no sexual rewards? The entire plan was more ridiculous than I'd previously thought.

"You're a friend of Jude's, and she introduced us when you helped us move two years ago. We got talking over carrying boxes and realized we had a lot in common."

"Sounds like a love story you'd tell your grandchildren when you're old."

Was he mocking me? I kicked his leg playfully under the table, and he burst out laughing. Yes, definitely mocking me.

"You have a better story?" I challenged.

He shrugged, playing for time. "You could say I brought your pizza, and you liked the stuffed crust so much you had to reorder. That's when you realized beneath the delivery uniform hid the man of your dreams." His eyes twinkled.

"That's the lamest story I've ever heard. I doubt anyone would believe it."

"Why?" He threw his hands up in mock exasperation while regarding me intently. "You don't believe you could find a diamond beneath a layer of sawdust?"

Was that a trick question?

"Maybe," I said, unsure where he was heading.

"Because I do. As hard as it might be for you to believe, I do." His voice dropped to a mere whisper. "I believe there's more to us than meets the eye, and if we're willing to take a second look, past first impressions, then we might just find a sparkle we were too blind to see before."

Why did I get the feeling he was talking about us? I stared at him, my heart beating against my chest so hard I almost feared it'd burst. His eyes turned all broody and intense again, regarding me with a depth of tenderness I had never seen before.

*The kind of tenderness that could bloom into love.*

I moistened my lips and turned away uncomfortably, seeking escape, if only for a few moments. When I turned back to him, he just smiled, the strange expression from earlier gone.

"Of course, the risk with second looks is that you might not like what you see at all, so...." He shrugged and trailed off, leaving the rest unspoken. In the silence, I watched him pop a grape into his mouth before I replied.

"Except I don't believe in second looks," I whispered. I wasn't even sure what came over me to challenge him.

"You don't?" He looked up, surprised. A stubborn line appeared on his otherwise smooth forehead. "I gather you're the first-impressions kind, then. No second chances."

I shook my head, unsure whether I was confirming his statement, or denying it. All my life I had been taught to remain unwavering and cold, never to cave in out of fear that if I let people get too close to me, the outcome might be ugly. People made mistakes that could rarely be rectified. They would always linger like a persistent stain that might fade over time, but would always be there.

"No second chances," I said, more to myself than to Chase.

"Are you serious?" he asked.

"I am. People don't change. If they make a mistake once, they'll repeat it, maybe even over and over again." I watched him lean back with a strange expression on his face—part puzzle, part curiosity. For once I wished I could just ask him to share his thoughts.

"I should leave." I grabbed my handbag and stood.

"Sure. Let me close up." No hesitation. No trying to change my mind. I was disappointed because, for some reason, I had hoped he'd try to keep me a little longer.

On our way home, we remained silent. Granted, my first impression of him hadn't been a good one, but by the end of the evening, my opinion had shifted. Only, I didn't want him to know. Not with all those tense moments between us and no clue as to what attracted me to him to such an extent. There had to be something else other than his appearance because, even though I had always been attracted to dark hair and pale eyes, my reaction to those had usually been more demure and less driven by my libido. He had stirred something deep inside me. I could only guess it was a need to be fulfilled.

However, there was something else, too. A longing to look at him when he wouldn't notice. A wish to get to know him—the real him—without being too apparent.

Chase pulled over on the other side of the road and killed the engine. I brushed a hand through my hair as I tried to fight the annoying part of me that wanted to stay just a little bit longer.

"Thanks," I mumbled, and was reaching for the door when his fingers curled around my arm gently, but with enough force to stop me.

"Laurie?" His voice indicated our conversation wasn't over. "Under different circumstances, I would ask you out on a date."

My heart did a somersault.

"The circumstances are as they are. It's just a job, and then we're done." My tone was supposed to be sharp, determined. Instead, all I managed was a croak filled with regret.

His eyes narrowed, sparkling with smoldering heat and the kind of determination I seemingly lacked.

"Then let me make you *feel* what could be between us, and you'll change your mind," Chase whispered, and let go of my arm.

Without so much as a glance back, I stumbled out of the car, back to my home, away from him and the one thing I shouldn't be feeling: attraction.

## Chapter 6

WHAT THE HELL was that all about?

I kept musing over Chase's words through the rest of the evening. And now I was still musing as I waited for Jude to finally emerge from her bedroom-based office once she finished typing up a new post for her blog.

"Okay, what's wrong? What did the jerk do beside take you home way too early?" Jude asked, plopping down on the sofa and almost landing in my lap. I moved aside to make room for her and regarded her, confused.

"Jerk?" I asked. "What are you talking about?" A glance at my watch showed it was just after 8 p.m. "It's hardly early."

She rolled her blue eyes. "Well, obviously, you're very

much confused and, judging from the glint in your eyes, very much horny, so I figured he probably got you all hot, and dropped you like a hot saucepan."

My jaw dropped. "Classy," I muttered. "I love your metaphors, although I'll have to admit that comparing me with a saucepan is a first. But no, I asked him to bring me home. That's it."

"Why would you do that?" Now it was her turn for her jaw to drop in shock, as if I had done something horrible. Finally, her lips curved into a lazy smile as comprehension kicked in.

"Did he or did he not make a pass at you? You haven't answered my question." Her eyes ripped a hole in my pretense.

I cringed. "Kind of."

"Good. He's playing you, and from the way you look, you're probably fed up with it and want him to make a move while your panties are still hot. I completely get you." She smiled mysteriously. "We've got to devise a battle plan if we're to beat him at his own game."

"Panties—what?" I shook my head. "Never mind."

Even though we had been best friends for ages, half the time I had no idea what Jude was talking about. Now was one of those times.

"So, let's get to strategizing," Jude said, ignoring me.

"He's my employee, not my poker adversary."

"He'd better not be, because with me on your side, he'll lose big time," Jude said. "Now tell me everything."

Still clueless as to what she was talking about, I related a quick recap of my meeting with Chase, leaving out all the double-entendres and the brooding looks and, most importantly, the touching, and his parting words.

"He didn't invite you in?" Jude asked incredulously, her brows drawn at me like I was lying to her.

"No," I said. "And I'm glad he didn't, because it would have been embarrassing, and, let's face it, I'm already embarrassing the crap out of myself by employing him to play my lover."

"Seems like he thinks you're relationship material."

Whoa, where did that one come from?

"What?" I laughed nervously. "Why would you come to such a conclusion?"

"It's pretty simple," Jude said in her teacher voice—the one she always used when she was in her element, aka talking about dating, sex, guys, or a combination of either of those. "Guys invite you in when they think you're a quick and easy lay or when you're in the friend zone. Either you've given him the impression you're one of those two, or he actually likes you and doesn't want to add you to the 'meaningless sex' pile because he believes more could develop between you. Given that he knows nothing about you, meaning you could be the biggest slut or the greatest saint on earth, I'd go with the second option. He thinks you're not 'meaningless sex' material. Does that make sense?"

No, it didn't. Not one bit.

"Your theory's faulty, because he's not a relationship kind of guy," I pointed out. "He didn't invite me in because he wants this job. We keep our communication limited to a strictly professional level."

Only, we hadn't. Some of his gestures had been too intimate, while his words had made me sense a deeper layer to them.

"If you think so." Jude smirked, which she always did when she didn't agree with me. "But I'm telling you, you're wrong. If he has enough money to buy himself the fast little number he's driving *and* a shack outside the city, surrounded by beautiful nature and hundreds of acres of land, he doesn't need your shitty-paying job, no offense."

"None taken," I mumbled. I hadn't seen it that way before, but she was right. Chase could afford an expensive car *and* an apartment in Los Angeles *and* a weekend house outside the city? It wasn't even rented. He had said he bought it as an investment.

Still, I wanted to tell her that her suggestion was silly, but then I noticed how quiet she had become. Suddenly, she jumped up and in three strides she reached the window, her back turned to me as she pulled the curtains aside and peered out onto the dark street.

"Switch off the lights," she commanded.

"What's—" I began, but she cut me off.

"Do it, Laurie."

I switched off the lights, bathing the room in complete darkness. A sense of discomfort suddenly gripped hold of me as I inched to the window, trying to peer over Jude's shoulder. Unfortunately, she was a few inches taller than I was and blocked my view of the street below.

"What's going on?" I whispered.

Jude didn't reply, but her rigid back and worried face showed her tension.

"Jude," I prompted. My voice betrayed a sharp edge.

"I think I saw someone loitering outside," Jude finally replied, her gaze still glued to the window, searching through the moonless night. It wasn't her words that worried me; it was her tone. That and the fact that we lived on the first floor. It would have been all too easy to break into the apartment through one of the windows.

"What do you mean by 'loitering'?" I whispered, and then tugged at her sleeve. "Let me see."

As she stepped aside, I scanned the street below. A streetlamp cast ominous shadows on the bushes on the other side of the road, but apart from a few parked cars, I saw nothing. Still, a shudder ran down my spine.

Streetlamps, with their dim light and flickering bulbs,

had often scared me as a child. I used to spend hours long past my bedtime staring at the one in our driveway, right below my bedroom window—where I had watched all the comings and goings, and my fair share of incidents no child should ever see.

To this day, streetlamps scared me because of the way the darkness around them seemed to swallow the light, giving refuge to lurking shadows. It was as if streetlamps were not only attracting and protecting bad people; they also seemed to reveal the dark side of humanity, the one that stayed hidden behind a smile during the day.

*Even the purest of hearts hides darkness in it, be it a single, silent drop or a raging hurricane. The heart might not know it until darkness descends, but by then it is lost forever in an ocean of shadows.*

I had learned that lesson the hard way.

Jude closed the curtains and switched on the lights. As my eyes slowly adjusted to the sudden brightness, I blinked several times.

"What did you see?" I asked, even though my conscious mind kept telling me there had been nothing out there. Probably just a trick of the light.

"Just—" Jude shook her head and sat down on the sofa, but her shoulders remained tense. "I thought I saw something stirring in the bushes."

"Probably the wind."

"Yeah." She didn't sound convinced. There was a short

pause. She wanted to believe—I could see it written all over her face—but something kept her back. Maybe intuition. Maybe an overactive imagination, the consequence of a hard day and too much stress.

"Something flickered," Jude added.

"Like a light bulb?"

"No. Something like a flash, like that of a keychain or something. I thought someone was standing behind a bush, searching the ground or something." She let out a shaky breath. "Just weird."

It was.

I frowned as my mind flicked through various explanations. "Maybe a cigarette lighter, or someone opened a window and the streetlamp reflected in it." It wouldn't have been the first time, though it usually happened in the stifling summer heat, when the relentless sun stood high in the sky, its light unobstructed by clouds.

"Probably." She still didn't sound convinced, but she was ready to drop it. She got up and pulled me with her to the kitchen. "It doesn't matter anyway. What matters is that you had your first official date today, and your fiancé is gorgeous." She drew the word out in a singsong, making me cringe. "A hot fiancé. Come on, we have to celebrate."

"He's not my fiancé, Jude," I said for the umpteenth time, only to be brushed off with a wave of her hand.

"Semantics, Laurie. Semantics. You know how I feel

about your quibbling over them."

I did.

Whenever I said something she didn't agree with, it was always open to *her* interpretation.

She retrieved a wine bottle from the upper shelf and poured it into two glasses, then handed me one. Her eyes twinkled as she raised her glass.

"To you for having met your gorgeous fiancé. And to me for being the perfect matchmaker ever," she said. "And here's to me again because I'm awesome."

I narrowed my eyes at her as she took a sip and raised her hand to stop me before I had a chance to reply.

"Oh, yeah, I almost forgot. I have great news." She sat up straight and brushed her hair back, suddenly nervous. "I am going to expand my business. My blog has caught the interest of a major TV network, and now they want me to appear in one of their morning shows once a week."

"Are you serious?"

She nodded, moisture glinting in her eyes. "It's a dream come true."

"Wow. That's huge." I clapped my hand over my mouth in surprise. "Which one?" I asked, surprised, genuinely happy for her.

"The one about unusual home decorating ideas." She squealed with delight. "I'm so glad you insisted I give it a try. I would never have done it, were it not for you."

"Jude, you're going to be a celebrity," I said, proud of her. She even looked the part, with her tall, toned body, blue eyes, and dark blonde hair. "You deserve everything. I'm so...so proud of you. Give me a hug."

I pulled her to me and engulfed her in a tight embrace.

"Yeah." She hesitated. "I don't mind being a celebrity as long as people see my talent because, one day, I want to furnish all the big department stores, TV studios, and maybe even the President's home."

I laughed at her enthusiasm. "Yeah, why not? You have what it takes." And I meant every word of it.

If someone could do it, then that person was Jude. The moment I saw her, I knew she was a star in the making, and now this was the proof I' been waiting for all along.

"You know what? We're not celebrating with this cheap wine." I took her glass away and put it back on the kitchen table. "This is the day you will always remember. You deserve the best cocktail in town. We should go out and *really* celebrate. My treat," I offered, even though my last money was being wasted on Chase's services. With no job prospects on the horizon, I'd be cleaned out in a month. But, damn, I wasn't going to crawl back to Waterfront Shore, even if it meant taking a job as a dog sitter.

"Love you. You're the best." Jude wrapped her arms around me and placed a hard kiss on my cheek, then jumped up to get dressed. The moment she disappeared, my phone beeped with a text message from Chase.

**I had fun today. We should do it again. What's the next step?**

I smiled.

*He had fun today. He wants to do it again.*

My heart fluttered like a wild hummingbird at the prospect of seeing him again, of hearing his deep voice, and proceeding to the next step. Never mind the fact that I was scared to death of what that next step might be.

Under different circumstances, I would have run. But not from Chase. Even though I didn't know him, I could feel his charm and ability to make everything sound intriguing working on me.

And intrigued I was.

A second later, Jude's statement about his interest in me echoed in the back of my mind. I shook it off, refusing to think about whatever that might mean and whether there might just be a trace of truth to it. There was no need to become obsessive about what he really thought of me, of whether he liked me more than just a friend would. And there was certainly not going to be any obsessing about whether Chase thought I was relationship material—

I groaned, irritated with myself, as I realized I had started to obsess again. Thinking about possibilities and wondering what Chase might consider to be our next step when there should be none was not acceptable.

Ignoring his question, my fingers flew over the touchscreen. He had a job to do, and that was all we'd ever focus on. In no way would I ever repeat the mistake of overanalyzing his words again.

**Compile a list per email of all the things we should know about each other.**
**Laurie**

One minute later, my phone beeped again.

**Consider it done. Can't wait to see yours first. ;)**

In spite of my clear resolutions, I found myself smiling. If I didn't know any better, I would have thought he was flirting. Thank God I had no time to follow my disturbing train of thought, because footsteps sounded in the hall. I pushed my phone back into my handbag just as Jude appeared in the doorway.

"Ready?" She beamed at me. On the way out, she made a big fuss of not taking her handbag with her, but I caught her squeezing several bills into her jeans pocket when she thought I wasn't looking.

Chapter 7

THREE DRINKS LATER, followed by the beginning of a pounding headache, and we were back in our apartment. Or, more precisely, I was back, because a guy had chatted up Jude, and I used the excuse to drive back home alone, leaving her at the bar for a little longer so she could enjoy herself. For the past half hour, I had been staring at the couple of lines on the computer screen, unsure what to put down on virtual paper. As it turned out, Chase had sent another message in which he *insisted* that I compile a list for him with all the things I thought he should know about me, like favorite food and the brand of toothpaste I used.

Things I liked to do in my spare time.

Hopes and dreams for the future.

Things so mundane, they should have posed no trouble at all. Only, after the first two questions, my mind had bottled up, unwilling to reveal so much as the usual time I woke up in the morning.

In spite of the chilly air coming from the air conditioning, a thin layer of sweat covered my back.

*Tell the truth, Hanson.*

*Fess up to the fact that you're alone, defeated, desperate, and ready to crawl back into the dangerous cocoon that was life at home. But remember that with sacrifice comes victory. And with victory comes freedom from all the bonds.*

*Freedom I needed and longed for.*

I had bottled everything up for so long, I didn't know how to be free. All those secrets I was carrying with me, never able to share them with anyone, had begun to hurt me to the core. My soul had been trapped in pain and the knowledge of having seen the kind of things I should never have seen. If I revealed to Chase only a fraction of the real me—enough for him to get to know me without being freaked out—then I could win.

And I had to win. Not next year, nor years after today. It had to be this month—before I turned twenty-three. I was going to win even if it meant cutting my heart open so Chase could see inside me.

The real me.

Better a stranger than the people I had once trusted, people who had turned out to be more different than I had ever imagined.

I set my chin and began to type, giving Chase all the basic information he needed, leaving out the most important facts, such as why I had to do what I had to do. Once I was finished, I sent off the list, happy with the fact that I was doing *something*. Finally making the difference I had always wished for but never had the guts to pursue. Soon my struggles would be over.

Finally, only one thing remained. I picked up my cell phone, my fingers hovering over the contact list and the one name I usually avoided calling like the plague. But today I had no choice. He had to be notified about my engagement. My finger swiped the screen and pressed the call button, and the line began to ring. Eventually, the one person who was responsible for most of the pain and pretense I had to go through picked up: my stepfather, Clint.

\*\*\*

I kept the call as short as possible and my news to a bare minimum. Once I was done, I sent off the email before I could change my mind, then went through the classified ads advertising jobs one more time...without much success.

With rejection emails cluttering my inbox, I was slowly beginning to think I was jinxed.

In the end, I gave up for the day and shut down my computer, ready to focus on the one thing I had been dreading all along: preparing myself for the event I had avoided for more than three years.

Three years during which I had kept running in the hope I might finally break free, only to find out I had no choice but to return and face the stuff of my nightmares.

Chapter 8

IT HAD BEEN a few days of hard preparations and panic attacks induced by the fear choking me. Eventually, the inevitable arrived.

"They're here," I whispered to Jude, even though they couldn't possibly hear me through the tinted glass of the limousine pulling up in front of our building.

"Laurie, look at me." Jude's hands squeezed my shoulders hard, forcing me to meet her determined gaze. "You're going to be okay. I'll make sure of that. I've got your back."

And she did. Just the day before, she had bought me a fake engagement ring, which I was wearing now. It had a small, pale blue aquamarine stone, and to the untrained eye, it almost looked like a diamond. According to Jude, it had been cheap, but judging from the way it sparkled, I wasn't so sure about that.

"Thanks." I almost choked on the word as I fought the urge to hide in her room and let her shield me from the world out there for the rest of my life. "I wish I didn't have to go through with this."

But there was no escape. My stepfather Clint was here, and with him his girlfriend of the year: Shannon, a tall blonde I only knew from phone calls and the pictures they had sent me last Christmas.

She looked about my age, but I could instantly sense something about her, a predatory trait that had managed to keep him interested in her for longer than the few weeks it usually took him to love and dump his girlfriends.

After my mother's death, I had often wondered how someone as devout as she had been all her life could have fallen for such a man-whore, and why she had granted him access to her wealth, leaving me in his care and to his mercy financially. Maybe, when she put that ridiculous clause in her will, she should have done the same thing for him. Instead, she had trusted him blindly in her belief that he'd uphold her values beyond her grave. Trusting he would always stay the same kind of man with a smile on his lips. If only she had looked deeper, past his tanned skin and soulful eyes, to notice the shadows in his soul. Maybe then she would have seen him for the kind of person he really was.

"Promise me that if anything happens, you'll remind me why I'm doing this. Why I put up with all his shit," I whispered to Jude, drawing the curtains.

"Sure," Jude said, her worried gaze scanning me up and down.

The seconds ticked by too quickly as they exited the limousine and Jude buzzed them in, a confident smile playing on her lips as she introduced herself as the roommate they had heard about but never met.

And then he stood before me. Dressed in his usual expensive gray striped suit, he oozed power and egocentric magnetism—the kind you usually observe in a crouching tiger.

"Laurie," Clint said. "I'm so happy to finally get to see my darling girl."

Even his voice was still as smooth and silky as I remembered. It took every inch of my willpower not to shrink back as his arms wrapped around my body and he pulled me to him.

I almost choked in his enthusiastic embrace and the force of his cologne. In the three years we hadn't seen each other, he had put on weight around the midriff, and his once dark hair had turned an attractive shade of salt and pepper that suited his tanned, lined face. He had aged well for a fifty-year-old, and in spite of the slight weight gain he looked in great shape, courtesy of the huge swimming pool and fitness area that he had built specifically for him so he could pursue his enthusiasm for looking good.

I tried to pull away politely, without much success. Luckily, Shannon cut in. "My turn, darling."

Clint released me and pointed to Shannon's figure, clad in a black designer dress that exposed half of her big fake bosom and long, thin legs. "Laurie, this is Shannon. She's wanted to meet you ever since I showed her pictures of you."

I cringed inwardly. "Nice to meet you," I said.

She shook my hand gingerly, and then pulled me to her in an awkward hug. Even her handshake was as weak as I suspected. Not much of a substantial character, I concluded.

"Look at you. You're so pretty." She smiled, revealing two strings of immaculate teeth, and wrapped her skinny arms around my waist, holding me at a safe distance. I could almost hear the "if only" echoing in the air between us while she took in every inch of me. I had heard that one before. If only I did something with my brown hair. If only I invested in some expensive designer clothes rather than walk around in my comfy jeans. The list went on and on.

"Thank you. You, too," I said.

She *was* very pretty—in an obvious kind of way. She seemed desperate to show off her beauty—both through her choice of clothes and through her body. Even from a distance I could clearly see she'd had a couple of things done: her lips were pursed in an unnatural pout; her nose looked too thin, almost frail, her chest too round and perky. The list went on.

"So, how long are you staying?" I only realized how rude I sounded the moment my words had left my mouth. But it was the only one question that mattered, because, in the end, I couldn't wait to get rid of them. Luckily for me, my visitors didn't seem to notice.

"Just for tonight," Shannon said, turning to Clint as though for approval. He nodded, and she continued, "We thought we might stop by. Tomorrow we'll be heading for Vegas two days before returning to Hawaii for sailing." She patted his arm. "He bought a new yacht. You have to see it. It's gorgeous."

Gambling, glitz, and glamour—Clint definitely knew how to do those things.

"Sounds great." Jude said with a saccharine smile on her lips that screamed sarcasm. "Why don't you guys make yourself comfortable while Laurie and I get you a drink?"

Without waiting for anyone's reply, she dragged me out the door to the kitchen and closed the door behind her. "Barbie seems nice," she said as she began to prepare her trademark café macchiato.

"Yeah."

They all played nice...until they thought Clint was all theirs. Then the claws came out, and with the claws came the bitchiness and the possessiveness and the drama. Clint was all theirs...only he wasn't. And when they finally realized he had played them all along and never meant to commit to any of them, they were in shambles.

I had watched it for years, vowing never to trust men or relationships in general. Men were like poison, slowly creeping into your soul and destroying you from within. Clint was the best example. I had done well without a man and I wanted it to stay that way, which was one of the reasons I would not let myself get too close to Chase.

"This one seems to be a keeper," Jude continued. "They've been together for—what?"

"One year."

Jude let out a low whistling sound. "A gold-digging keeper."

In spite of my gloomy mood, I found myself smiling. "He'll get rid of her soon," I said.

"I'm not so sure about that." Jude smirked. "Did you see the way he looks at her? She's almost our age. And he bought a yacht. I bet it was to impress her."

"Maybe." I shrugged and placed a few doughnuts on a plate, then set the plate on the coffee tray. Usually, I wasn't one to play the hostess type, serving coffee and cake, but I could tell Shannon was a worshipper of the no-carb diet. If

I had to endure a few days in their presence, I figured I might as well try to have fun doing it.

"Come on before they come chasing after us." I grabbed the tray and headed back into the lions' den.

Chapter 9

"IT'S A BEAUTIFUL place," Shannon said upon my entering. "Thanks for inviting us into your home. To be honest, we didn't expect it."

Neither did I, but life was full of surprises.

Usually, I didn't agree to meet up, and particularly not in my apartment. But after my call and the brief announcement of my engagement, Clint had been unusually persistent until I caved in eventually in the hope that by agreeing I'd have him off my back soon enough.

"You're welcome." I placed the tray on the coffee table and began handing out dessert plates and coffee cups, all the while watching Shannon's dismal expression as she spied the doughnuts.

"Have one. They're the best in town." I handed the plate with chocolate-covered doughnuts toward Clint, who helped himself to one, and then turned my gaze to Shannon. Beneath her tan, her face had turned an ashen shade, and I figured in her head she probably believed even *looking* at sugar would make her fat.

"Great." She drew out the word beyond recognition as she stared at the doughnut like the devil was about to tempt her.

For a second, silence ensued, and then she turned to Clint. "Darling, think about your cholesterol. I'm sure Laurie won't be upset, since she didn't know."

"Sorry, Laurie," Clint said, handing his plate back to me. "Doctor's orders."

She shot me a triumphant smile. No arguing, no dictating to him what to do, just plain old manipulation. She was definitely smarter than the rest of his floozies. I had to give her that. I decided to play along.

"It's okay. It's not like I made them myself." I took a sip of my hot coffee, ignoring the stinging burn. "Why the sudden need to see me?"

Clint laughed, the sound embarrassingly fake. "Why, do I need a reason to see my only daughter? Congratulations are in order for your recent engagement."

*Stepdaughter*, I wanted to add. And without my mother's money, he would have had nothing. Been nothing. He would have still been working in car sales rather than living off her wealth and luxury, of which I had nothing.

I smiled and remained silent, my gaze piercing him. He shifted uncomfortably on the sofa, and his arm went around Shannon's waist, pulling her just a little bit closer than she already was, which was basically on his lap. His piercing brown eyes focused on me once more, and I wondered why he kept looking at me like that.

Strange.

Downright creepy.

Cold as ice.

A chill glided down my spine, but I didn't shift. Didn't even blink. Nothing to betray just how much he unnerved me. There were shadows under his eyes, I realized. The rhythmical tapping of his fingertips on his thigh suggested that he was nervous. But why?

"So, apart from your recent developments." He cleared his throat. "There's another reason why I wanted to see you. Why *we* wanted to see you, Laurie."

*What now?*

I swallowed down the sudden lump in my throat. My eyes went several times back and forth between them, until my glance came to rest on the large diamond ring on Shannon's finger. Either she had kept it out of my vision until now, or I hadn't seen it.

My heart lurched in my chest.

As if noticing my lingering gaze, he continued, "Shannon and I want to get married soon. We need to sort out your mother's last wishes, seeing that you're engaged, too."

I stared at him, for a moment struck speechless by my bewilderment. "You're getting married?" I asked, unable to hide my shock. For some reason, I had always thought he'd stay single—like he had done for so many years. I had expected him to congratulate me on my engagement and my engagement only, not to pop over with Shannon and announce their plans. My stomach twisted as I realized the full implications of what he was about to do.

"We've been engaged for a few months now," Clint said, his gaze searching Shannon's as though to seek her approval or confirmation. "We didn't tell you earlier because the right moment never presented itself. Besides, we won't be making a big deal out of it."

It was a lie.

As a child, I had been a keen observer of human behavior, and Clint had been a worthy research subject. I could see it in the way his gaze kept darting around that he hadn't been engaged for long. He probably barely knew her.

I had suspected something like that would happen, but the truth hurt nonetheless. He was moving on, with a woman half his age, in my mother's mansion. It had been years since her death and I wanted to see him happy, but what I couldn't cope with was the fact that Shannon would be mistress of the place that had belonged to my mother. The place she had inherited from her rich family. The place where I had grown up and once considered home.

It wasn't fair.

Nodding, I swallowed hard and kept the air trapped in my lungs until they began to burn. Only then did I exhale and turn back to Clint, fully aware that congratulations were due.

"Fine. What do you want?" My voice was calm and steady, but underneath I was seething.

"Like I said, we need to talk, considering your recent developments," he repeated.

"You mean my engagement?"

He nodded gravely, his smile gone. "I want you to have what your mother meant for you," he said slowly. "The fiancé you mentioned"—he glanced at Shannon with a look that said he wasn't convinced I wasn't making him up…which I was, but the action angered me nonetheless— "we'd like to finally meet him."

"Have you set a wedding date yet?" Shannon asked.

"Not yet. He's very busy, and then there's my job and the fact that we haven't found our own place yet." I trailed off and waved my hand as if it didn't matter.

Shannon nodded sympathetically, even though judging from the look of her long, manicured nails, she had probably never worked a day in her life, or had to find her own place rather than sponge off some old-timer.

"He's an actor," Jude said. I shot her a warning look, but she turned away, ignoring me. "Like so many other actors, he came to LA to make it big and he did it." She smiled, like a proud mother hen. Like she had anything to do with his success. "He's very famous and sought-after, even has a nice place outside the city. Laurie's been staying over a lot of weekends lately." She laughed. "I hope they use protection, because you're way too young to be a grandma yet, Sharon."

"It's Shannon," she replied with a hint of arrogance, and I bit my tongue to stop myself from laughing at her venomous expression.

"Well, don't keep him a stranger. We want to know everything about him," Clint said.

"That's great, because Mr. Tall and Beautiful is coming over tonight, isn't he, Laurie?" Jude grinned at me, urging me to play along. "Like he's been doing every day."

Which was kind of the truth. During the past few days, he had stopped over a few times. While I had refused to venture out with him in order to avoid being alone with him and dodge the kind of situation I had encountered at his cottage, Jude's presence had done nothing to dampen the attraction I felt toward him.

"Laurie?" Jude prompted. "When are you seeing

Chase?" I shot her a dirty look and she raised her eyebrows at me, mouthing a *what?*

Obviously, I had no idea what his plans were for tonight, because we had arranged for him to be on duty tomorrow, in case I couldn't convince Clint that meeting my fiancé wasn't a good idea.

Jude and I had talked about this at length and we had agreed that she should keep her mouth shut—not encourage my stepfather to continue poking in my private life.

A task she had failed at miserably.

"Uh. He might not. You never know with him," I said. "He's busy this week. He always is." A suspicious frown crossed Clint's face. I hated his smugness and the fact that he constantly thought he was superior to everyone else.

"But he texted you this morning," Jude insisted. "He said he was looking forward to meeting your family."

Clint's frown deepened as he regarded me closely.

I took a deep breath and let it out slowly. "You know what? I think I'll call him right away." I jumped up and headed for my bedroom, calling over my shoulder, "I'll be right back," before I could change my mind.

Behind me, I heard Jude saying, "She might be a while."

Her crystalline laughter followed me to my room until I closed the door and slumped on the bed, burying my head in my palms.

What the heck was I doing? Chase could play my fiancé only for so long, and then my lies would be exposed. And then what? I would lose everything. Everything that belonged to my mother.

I retrieved my cell phone from the bedside table and dialed Chase's number, ignoring the warning bells that hadn't stopped ringing in my head since Clint's arrival.

*Take it one step at a time.*

I needed Chase now. He couldn't let me down. With each ring, my heart beat stronger until he finally picked up his phone.

"Hey, you," I said, my throat constricting.

"Laurie?" A pause, then, "Are you okay?"

"Yes. Great." My voice betrayed my stress, and I forced myself to take a long breath before continuing. "They're here. They want to see you. I need you to come over now." I cringed inwardly at how fake my cheerfulness sounded. Not natural at all. If I continued like that, Clint was bound to see through my bluff.

"I can do that," Chase said. "Where are you?"

"At home," I whispered. "Let's meet at a restaurant in an hour. I can't have them here. I just can't."

"Sure. I'll make a reservation and text you the details." His voice dropped lower. "Are you okay?"

"I'll feel better once you're here." I bit my lip hard to stop myself from revealing just how much better his arrival

123

would make me feel. "And Chase? Please don't make a reservation at that strip bar you took me to."

He laughed, and for a moment I imagined him on the phone, the skin around his eyes crinkling the way it always did when he smiled, his eyes sparkling with something I could never pinpoint. The sound of his laughter echoed in my ear long after I hung up.

I realized it was the part I liked most about him.

*Chapter 10*

"FORGIVE ME FOR asking but, fuck, how old is she?" Chase whispered the moment we caught a moment alone. We were having dinner in a nearby restaurant. Chase had excused himself, claiming to have to make an urgent phone call while I needed to visit the bathroom. And now we were standing in the corridor leading to a picturesque backyard with lanterns and several empty tables. Given that it was still early, the restaurant—a small family-run operation—was almost empty, giving us privacy.

"I don't know. Maybe nineteen, twenty-two tops. She's definitely younger than I am." I shrugged, even though I actually cared. My mother had thought the world of Clint. That he brought his first tramp home a few weeks after her funeral had bothered me for years. That they had been getting younger and he was marrying one of them only managed to enrage me even more.

"What the fuck is he doing with someone like her?" Chase asked.

"He's screwing his brains out."

"Probably chasing after his second youth or something."

"More like the third." I smiled, liking him even more for being different. Of course, things could change, but for the time being I settled on believing Chase shared my morals and beliefs.

"And he's sullying my mother's memory," I whispered, so low that Chase wouldn't hear me. The memories were few and faint, and as time passed, the picture of her weakened. The ring of her voice inside my head had quieted a long time ago, the silence a shadow of her vivacious self. I had been ten years old when she died. During the following eight years I had been in my stepfather's care, I had watched, and seen, observed, and struggled.

"I'm sorry. It must be so hard for you," Chase said, his tone sincere.

"You have no idea." For a moment our eyes connected, and something passed again between us. My chin began to quiver, and my throat went dry as his big hand moved around my neck, and he ever so gently drew me to him. He was so tall I barely reached his chin.

I pressed my cheek against the coarse fabric of his shirt, letting it chafe my skin, and inhaled his intoxicating scent. His height and the hardness of his muscles had been intimidating me ever since I met him, but under the circumstances they felt right, beckoning me to touch them.

"Laurie." His deep voice was hoarse, reverberating with something dark and meaningful, as his thumb moved beneath my chin, coaxing my head up to meet his gray-blue gaze. In the semi darkness, his lashes made his eyes shimmer dark-blue like a perilous river forging its way through a valley and stones. We were so close, I could feel his hot breath on my lips, barely an inch away, and yet too far. Something twitched within me, and the deep pull I had felt before returned, settling low in the pit of my stomach and traveling between my legs.

*He's a man. Sooner or later, he'll want the one thing you can't give him.*

I would never trust a man again.

The voice of reason hit me a moment before I realized I wanted to taste him, but, more than that, I wanted to run. He unleashed feelings inside me—a strange kind of want—and I didn't know what they meant. All I understood was that deep inside I craved his kisses. I craved melting in his embrace, mouth against mouth, skin against skin, fire burning through us.

I realized he was like fire, and if I didn't stop this, I was going to get burned.

Clearing my throat, I averted my gaze and pulled out of his embrace. His face remained blank, but his eyes betrayed his displeasure.

"I'm sorry, I—" I moistened my lips and straightened my clothes, as if to ward off any attraction I felt for him.

"There's nothing to feel sorry about," Chase whispered. "You're not ready, and I'm not going to push you."

He didn't need to. His mere presence was temptation enough.

I smiled bitterly, keeping my thoughts to myself. "Thanks."

"You said your family was old-fashioned. Clint doesn't look very old-fashioned to me."

He was curious. Everyone would be, given the circumstances. I knew the question would come eventually, but I didn't expect it so soon.

"He's not," I said briskly in the hope that Chase would drop the topic.

"Why did you lie to me, then?" he asked.

I looked up, expecting fury, but there was only curiosity. "I wasn't sure you'd understand."

He frowned. "Why the need for all of this?" he persisted. "They seemed to accept our engagement just fine."

"Look." I hesitated as I sorted through my thoughts.

Chase had turned out to be a nice person, but I couldn't trust him. "Can we talk about it another time?"

*Maybe never?*

I raised my gaze to meet his, and I almost choked seeing the hurt in his eyes. One rejection had been bearable; two were one too many. And then his lips bent into the beginning of a smile that lit up his face.

God, I loved it when he smiled.

"You owe me dinner…for all I'm doing tonight," Chase said.

"What? I'm paying for this one already, so, technically, you owe me." I smiled, thankful for the change in topic.

"I'll gladly pay if only you turn up." He brushed his thumb over my cheek and trailed it to the back of my neck, settling there. For a second, I thought he'd pull me to him again, and I almost forgot to breathe in the hope he'd go for it, knowing this time I wouldn't deny him. But Chase didn't follow my brain's plea; he just stared at me, a strange smile playing on his gorgeous lips.

"You're a mystery, Laurie, you know that?"

I moistened my lips, both mesmerized and threatened by his proximity. He was leaning in too close for comfort, his breath too warm and appealing to ignore. In a bold moment, I pushed up on my toes and placed a soft kiss on his lips. It was barely a second, but enough to send a jolt of pleasure through me.

"Ah, the tease." Chase arms reached for my waist, but I was faster. Laughing, I dashed past him down the corridor and into the eating area, faintly aware of his steps following close behind.

The magnitude of what I had done only hit me the moment I sat down and looked into Jude's inquiring face and her widening eyes, glistening with realization. She pulled out her cell phone and began typing furiously. An instant later, Chase appeared, and my phone vibrated, signaling a text message. Ignoring his heated gaze, I read the text.

**You were in there forever. What did you two do? Tell me it involved a lot of tongue.**

I shook my head at Jude, and she narrowed her eyes at me. Then she began to type again. This time, Chase pulled out his phone and peered up at Jude. She didn't believe me so naturally, being Jude, she had to seek other sources to dig up the truth. Chase threw me a sideways glance and then winked at Jude.

*Oh, god.*

Didn't he know he was stoking fire with fire?

I felt like sinking into the floor and praying for the earth to swallow me whole.

Jude's expression turned into one of triumph as she

pushed her cell phone back into her handbag and waved the service personnel over, demanding another round of drinks.

"How's the job hunting going?" Clint addressed me after the waiter had topped up my glass. I took a large gulp and let the vile, sour taste of red wine travel down my throat, barely able to hide my grimace.

*Anything to get me through the evening.*

"It's doing great," Jude said. "In fact, Laurie has a few very promising opportunities lined up. We can't decide." She laughed, and Shannon joined in politely, her eyes focused on me like a hawk's.

"Is that why you haven't cashed the last few checks I sent you?" Clint asked.

I nodded, more confident than I was feeling. "Yeah, something like that," I mumbled, and took another gulp of my wine, downing my glass. The waiter hurried over for a refill. Even though my brain screamed out a warning, I didn't stop him.

My credit cards were maxed out to the limit. The bank had already called to inquire about my ability to start repaying my student loan, and I had started to feel embarrassed about the fact that Jude had started paying more than half our rent a long time ago. I hadn't cashed Clint's checks because I didn't want the money, not because I didn't need it.

"Maybe you should put your pride aside when it comes

to your finances," Clint said.

"Darling. We talked about this, remember?" Shannon said warningly, but he brushed her off with a wave of his hand.

"No, she's old enough to deal with it," Clint said, turning to me. "We know about your troubles and the fact that you haven't been able to find a good job since leaving college. We've had phone calls from various credit card companies, people asking about you." The way he said it, he made me sound like I had borrowed money from the local mafia.

I rolled my eyes.

"You know we're here to help, Laurie," Clint continued. "And if you want to get back on your feet on your own, then that's fine. But living here on your own with no support isn't going to help you do that. Move back home. Start working for the company."

"Just for a year," Shannon cut in. "Until you've paid off your debts."

My hand clutched at the wine glass for support like it was my safe railing as my face caught fire.

"I'm fine. Like I said before, I need my independence."

Trust Clint to start washing my dirty laundry in public in front of the one guy I actually liked. I caught Chase's expression from the corner of my eye and almost tumbled under the table, mortified. His eyes were cast downward, his face rigid and unreadable, his mouth framed by two hard lines.

"We want you back home," Clint insisted, adding firmly, "where you belong."

"Only until you sort yourself out," Shannon cut in again, this time with a worried smile. She probably meant well, but in my rising fury I couldn't see past the fact that she had no idea what she was talking about. She had no idea what it meant to actually *want* to work for your money.

"I don't see that happening any time soon," I said with enough determination to hush even Clint.

Uncomfortable silence ensued. Sensing a change in the atmosphere, I took another gulp of my drink. I could almost taste the tension in the air, wafting between Clint and me the way it always did when we head-butted.

I didn't want Chase to see me like that because it wasn't the real me, but I just couldn't help myself around Clint. He brought out the worst in me.

"But he just wants to help you, Laurie," Shannon said, obviously eager to resume the conversation. "You should—"

I cut her short. "Stay out of this, Shannon. I'm not returning to Waterfront Shore."

*No matter what. It would be stupid to believe his lies.*

"You've always been too stubborn for your own good." Clint heaved an exasperated sigh. "Just like your mother.

We'll talk about this later."

"Great, but nothing you could possibly say will change my mind." I bit my tongue hard to keep back a snarky remark.

Chase squeezed my hand under the table, his warm touch coloring my mood a darker shade of grim. I yanked my hand away and waved the waiter to bring another bottle of wine. By the time we finished dinner, I was a giggly mess and hanging onto Chase's arm.

"Laurie," a deep, sexy voice rumbled in my ear. "I'll take you home, okay?"

"But I don't want to go home," I slurred, my head spinning, and not in a good way. "I want to get away. Far, far away."

"You don't know what you're talking about."

I giggled. No, he didn't know what *he* was talking about, which was why he didn't know that we both had to run.

*No turning back. Just keep on running...until we're safe.*

I giggled again and flinched at the pangs of pain shooting through my head, traveling right into my stomach. The night around us spun faster and faster as I was tucked into the back seat of a car and driven away.

"Get some sleep, and you'll be okay tomorrow."

I opened my eyes to regard the sexy stranger whose beautiful voice kept caressing my most secret spots, and I smiled up at him. His fingers gently brushed my hair out of my face and settled on my cheek. I leaned into his soft touch, wondering why he couldn't see the truth the way I did. Why couldn't he just see past the shadows of the human soul?

"Go away," I whispered. "Go away as quickly as you can."

*Before it's too late,* I added in my mind, but the words died on my lips as I closed my eyes and fell into oblivion. The last thing I remembered was the soft touch of his hand on my cheek.

Chapter 11

THE CATCHY POP tune blared through the room, penetrating my head like a sharp blade. Groaning, I turned and flinched as a hard throb began to pound against the walls of my brain, making me want to hide under the sheets and never come out again. Only, at some point, the pounding became so unbearable, I was forced to leave the safety of my cocoon and venture into the late morning sun.

"Good morning, sunshine," Jude sang from her kitchen stool, looking up from her computer screen. She clapped the screen shut, bathing the kitchen in heaven-sent silence, and pushed a warm cup of black coffee across the counter toward me. I wrapped my hand around it and downed it in three big gulps.

Only then did I manage a husky, "Thanks."

"You look like shit." Jude pointed at my crumpled, oversized shirt.

"You've just summed up the way I feel." I slumped onto a stool and placed my elbows on the table, my gaze already searching for my next caffeine fix.

Jude chuckled and refilled my cup, then went on to make me an egg omelette, because she was a firm believer in the importance of eating breakfast, which had always been one of the few things she and I kept arguing about.

"What a night, huh?" She placed a plate with some yellowish pulp in front of me and pushed a slice of toast into my hand, silently commanding me to eat up. Just looking at the yellow mush made my stomach turn. I began moving chunks around my plate, but didn't dare take a bite in case my nausea flared up.

Great night…if only I could remember more than a few blurry pictures and pieces of broken conversation.

"Eat up," she said, "or would you rather I fed you?"

"Yes, Mom." I pushed a chunk of egg white into my mouth and forced myself to chew slowly, realizing it was quite nice.

"It wasn't as bad as I had expected," I said, referring to the evening before.

"I was being sarcastic, Laurie," she exclaimed. "It was horrendous. One of the most cringe-worthy evenings of my life." She shook her head and let out a huff of air. "I was counting the seconds until we could get out of there. I'll tell you up front—I'll never ever do that again."

Trust Jude to tell it as it was. No sparing my feelings.

"You were embarrassed," I said, faintly remembering thinking something along those lines.

"Are you kidding me? I was embarrassed for *you*. If my stepfather talked to me like that in front of my so-called fiancé, I would have spewed fire at him."

I had no idea what Clint had said, but I could only imagine it must have been awful if Jude felt that way. She had always been on my team.

"Was it that bad?" I suppressed a smile.

"Bad? Are you kidding me? Try disastrous. Completely humiliating. You should have seen Chase's face. He was mortified."

I shook my head, unsure what she was referring to. The only thing I remembered was Clint talking about me going home while I wished I could sink into the bottom of my drink and drown in it.

"No wonder we couldn't pry you off the wine bottle. You don't even like wine," she continued, oblivious to my thoughts. "Now I see why I can't possibly let you move back home."

I smiled at her weak attempt at infusing humor. "They'd turn me into an alcoholic," I said, wondering what the heck

Clint had said.

"Exactly. And then we'd have to go together to rehab, because there's no way I'd let you go alone." She leaned over the table and grabbed my hand, forcing me to look at her. "While you were asleep, I mixed you my top-secret hangover cocktail."

She went over to the fridge and filled a glass of green liquid, then handed me the blend with an encouraging smile. "Drink up. Trust me, you'll feel better in no time. *This* is the only cure that will beat the mother of all hangovers."

I eyed it warily, then smelled it. Faintly, I could detect the scent of green tea, kale, and cucumber.

"Do I really have to?" I said, taking a tender sip.

"It will help you rehydrate. Now drink up. You'll need it." Her expression turned serious again. "Chase wants to talk to you."

*Oh, god.*

Groaning, I buried my head in my hands as I realized the magnitude of the situation. I almost never consumed alcohol, meaning I had absolutely no immunity against it. My threshold was basically nonexistent. From the few times I had been drunk in my entire life, I knew I was horrible while under the influence. My speech was slurred, and I said the most ludicrous things.

"How did I even get home?" I asked, looking up, eager

to change the subject.

"We drove you."

I didn't need to ask who "we" was to know the answer.

"Tell me you didn't let him tuck me into bed."

Jude's face remained all wide-eyed innocence. "What was I supposed to do? Do you think I'm a bodybuilder or something? You're too heavy to carry."

I stared at her. No way was I going to discuss my weight issues. Yes, my employment situation and tendency to comfort eat had caused me to pile on a few layers of fat, but it was no big deal. Nothing a few extra sessions at the gym couldn't solve.

"At least I'm still wearing my clothes. That should count for something," I muttered to myself, then looked up with renewed interest. I paused before asking, "What did I say?"

"Nothing." Jude shook her head, her expression a blank mask. The high ring in her voice didn't fool me, though.

"Jude, what did I say?"

She sighed, and in that instant I knew I could never see Chase again, not after the embarrassing performance he must have witnessed the previous night.

The only thing more embarrassing than an embarrassing performance is having too many nasty thoughts about other people in your head and not knowing which one you actually spoke out aloud.

"I'm going out." I jumped up and grabbed my plate,

placing it in the sink on my way out, leaving Jude's hangover concoction unfinished.

Jude followed me. "Where are you going?"

"I don't know where I'm going. Just out."

"Why?"

"Because this is too much. I thought I could deal with this all—with Clint, with—" I choked on the words *the past*. After a few years away from home, I had thought I'd put enough physical and emotional distance between the past and myself to react in a more detached manner, but last night's disaster had shown that I was nowhere near detached. Seeing that the present was just as awful, I couldn't descend back into the abyss that had once been my life.

With a shrug, I ignored Jude's stare and forced myself to take a few gulps of her self-made smoothie, which didn't taste as bad as it looked.

"Laurie, you can't leave. Clint's coming over in an hour," Jude said imploringly. "I know the guy's a pain in the ass, but Shannon called to inquire about you. Apparently, they're leaving today and want to see you before they head to the airport. It's just for five minutes."

"No way." A sarcastic snort escaped my throat. Even if he took the next plane back home, he'd never be completely gone. But Jude didn't know. No one did.

"You said you wanted to help," I said. "Please call them

back and tell them it was nice seeing them, but I'm not available. If they persist, tell them I'm busy and I won't be able to talk for the next week or so. Please. I promise I'll make it up to you."

I closed the door, then buried myself under the covers when my cell rang from an unknown number. Figuring whoever was calling would leave a message if it was important, I placed the cell phone on my nightstand and was preparing myself to go back to sleeping off my headache when the doorbell rang.

*Please, no.*

Was there no hope for peace in my own home?

Heaving an exasperated sigh, I sat up when chatter carried over and Jude called my name. With a groan, I pulled the covers over my head, ignoring her. Seconds later, the door was thrown open.

"Laurie," Jude said. "You need to get up. Someone wants to talk to you." Her voice carried a hint of worry.

"Who is it?" I asked from under the covers. "If it's Clint, tell him I have no time for him and his Barbie."

"It's not him. It's Clint's attorney."

"What?" I asked, surprised, and pushed the sheets back. "What does he want?" For the life of me, I couldn't fathom why someone like *him* would want to meet with someone like *me*.

She shrugged, signaling that she had no idea. "You

should talk with him, though. He said it's urgent and that he can't discuss any details with me because it's confidential."

"Awesome. Just what I needed." I exhaled slowly when another pang of pain shot through my head. "Tell him I'll be ready in a minute."

"Sure."

The door closed. Groaning, I sank under the covers. Of all the times in my life, why the heck would Clint's oldest friend and attorney choose today to pay me an unsolicited visit?

I counted to ten, then changed quickly into clean clothes and pulled my hair into a ponytail.

There was no point in applying makeup, and certainly no need to get rid of the scowl on my face. I had never made a secret of not liking him. Guys like him were sharks, and in particular those who worked for Clint. I decided I'd listen to whatever he had to say, then get him the hell out of our apartment so I could return to my bed to sleep off the pounding in my head.

Chapter 12

ALDWIN WAS A little stumpy guy with a bald head and a sharp chin that was emphasized by a thin goatee. He looked harmless enough, but he had the keenest eyes I had ever seen in a person. To say I had never trusted the guy was an understatement. Maybe my utter dislike of him could be attributed to the fact that he seemed to hang out with Clint on a frequent basis, always openly boasting about his victories—both in relation to young women and to various trials he always seemed to win. Aldwin was—simply put—an unpleasant man.

Like a salesman eager to flog off any product for the highest price possible, he was out to win with no regard for who ended up hurt or broke along the way. He had no sense of justice, which was ironic, considering he was supposed to be a man of the law. Helping others search for fairness wasn't his thing. I knew him as someone whose craving for money and building connections had always exceeded his moral understanding or ethnic views.

So, not surprisingly, I left the sanctuary of my bedroom and met with Jude in the hall with a fake smile plastered across my lips and pretty low expectations.

"Aldwin," I greeted him.

"Miss Hanson, thanks for seeing me," he said in his irritatingly high voice, which always made me cringe. He was standing near the door, his hand clutching at a briefcase, his eyes fixed on Jude hungrily. "May I invite you to walk with me to discuss a rather trivial matter?"

Trivial?

Then why the heck wouldn't he just call, like normal people? But in Aldwin's terms, "trivial" meant a lot of things.

"Okay." I inclined my head. "But please keep it short. I'm not in the mood for discussing any sort of matter. I have important business to tend to."

Which was a lie, but he didn't need to know that. My lie was supposed to ensure he kept the meeting as short as possible because, God knew, Aldwin could talk for hours. Upon grabbing my jacket from the rack, I caught Jude's "you've got to tell me everything" glance. And then she closed the door behind us, and I was left alone with the shark.

"It's a beautiful day, isn't it?" Aldwin began. "Times like this remind me how lucky we really are to be able to experience sunshine every day."

A beautiful day? Was he joking?

The sky was clouded, the sun hidden behind thick clouds. From the look of it, it would start to rain any time soon. I was ready to bet my nonexistent wages that it was his standard introduction speech to melt the ice before he started to discuss "trivial" matters.

"What do you want from me?" I asked and stopped, barely able to hide my irritation and distaste for the man.

"I want you to have what your mother meant for you," he said, repeating the exact same words as Clint. He'd probably received a transcript of the previous evening, I thought. "Clint…your stepfather and I have discussed your engagement at great length. He's so happy for you."

I snorted inwardly.

*That* I doubted very much.

"As am I," he continued in a fake-sincere voice. "Those are important developments, Laurie, which are aggravated by the fact that your stepfather will wed soon, too. Considering the fact that your mother didn't take into account a few things, such as to what should happen when your stepfather re-marries—" The fact that he chose the word "when" rather than "if" didn't escape me, but I let it slip. "—we had to make a few adjustments to the contract to benefit both you and Clint."

"What are you talking about? What adjustments? Clint and I had a verbal agreement. He keeps my mother's estate, meaning all of it, while I get the letters once I'm engaged." Frowning, I stared at him, my gaze cold as ice.

"In order to fulfil your *verbal* contract, you no longer have to be engaged." He paused for effect, and I almost breathed out, relieved...until I caught the malicious glint in his eyes. "We expect you to be legally married before your twenty-third birthday."

Was changing terms without the other party's consent even legal? After all, Clint and I had a verbal agreement, and that was just as binding as a written one.

If only I could prove it.

As if sensing my bewilderment, Aldwin nodded. "I understand your confusion, Miss Hanson. Your mother was very specific in her last will. She wanted Clint to have her money and insisted in her testament that you shall get her letters before you turn twenty-three. The condition was that you're not unattached, which, to me, means officially wedded."

He smiled, his eyes glinting with pretend kindness. "However, Clint and I have come to agree that, being her child, you're entitled to a quarter of her liquid assets, even if she didn't intend you to have it."

The way he said it, he made it sound like my mother was the evil witch and Clint a complete altruist.

"I'm sure she had a good reason," I found myself saying before I could stop myself.

Clint's smile froze on his lips, and the kindness in his eyes disappeared. "Anyway, seeing that your stepfather will remarry soon, we have drawn a new contract to avoid a future domestic dispute that might involve finances, may it come from you, or your future husband. We want to settle the issue once and for all."

"I do not want his money," I whispered so low I wasn't sure he heard me, emphasizing each word. Getting my mother's letters was the sole reason for my fake engagement. It had never been about money, and Clint knew it. Mother had always warned me never to take it, and I chose to believe her.

"Excuse me. What did you say?" Aldwin said, stunned. I stared at him as the penny finally dropped. Clint was scared Chase might insist that I claim my legal share of my mother's fortune. A pang of rage surged through me.

"I said, I don't want the money, and neither does my fiancé," I repeated. "I'm fulfilling my mother's last wish by being engaged by the time I turn twenty-three, which will be in just a few days, as I'm sure you're aware. I'm willing to give up my rights to a quarter of my mother's wealth in exchange for the letters. But I want them now." I stared him down, holding his hard glance. "That's all I want."

Aldwin drew a sharp breath. "Are...you sure?"

"Yes." I nodded.

"Miss Hanson, I'm afraid that's not quite possible." He moistened his lips and smiled the kind of smile that didn't reach his eyes. "You see, the terms of your mother's will were pretty clear. Being engaged isn't enough. You have to be married to fulfill the conditions of both getting the money and receiving the letters."

"But...." I struggled for words. How many times did I have to tell the guy that I didn't want any money? Just the letters. Why was it so hard to understand?

"But Clint and I made a verbal agreement years ago. He said I would get the letters if I got engaged. There was no mention of marriage."

"He's changed his mind," Aldwin said, then dropped his voice conspiratorially. "Miss Hanson, he's so happy for you and convinced of your love that he insists you marry. After all, time passes so quickly, and he wants to be sure that a man can take care of you and loves you for who you are rather than for your inheritance. Clint is convinced that your fiancé is a fine man. True love, without a doubt. His words, not mine. He has only your best interests at heart."

I stared at him.

Was he for real?

Clint didn't have my best interests at heart. In fact, I doubted he even cared whether I was dead or alive. Clint was trying to pay me off now, before Chase could persuade me to sue his ass to get my family inheritance. My mother's money had been passed down through generations, and my mother's mental state had been more than questionable at the time she wrote her will. Any judge would have been more than sympathetic hearing my case. I knew this because several legal firms had written to me to offer me their services.

"Of course." I laughed weakly, suddenly faint, and jutted my chin out. "Tell Clint that my fiancé and I will walk down the aisle on time. Now, if you'll excuse me, we have an appointment today. It's for a cake tasting, and that is one we can't miss. Please send him my regards."

"What about the contract I've drawn up? Will you be accepting the money?" His tone rang with fear. I wouldn't have been surprised to find his hairy back slick with sweat.

I laughed inwardly, enjoying my proverbial grip on his balls. "There is no need for a contract, considering that I will not accept." I gave him my most confident smile. "Thanks for meeting with me, Aldwin. It's been a pleasure."

Turning my back on him, I walked away from Aldwin and rounded a corner. Away from his curious gaze, I stopped and pressed my hand against my mouth as I fought hard to catch my breath.

"Fuck. Fuck. Fuck," I muttered, unable to control the anger and jabbing pain rising inside me. Now I was in real trouble. Contrary to whatever Aldwin and Clint thought, it really wasn't about the money, and it never would be.

My mother had wanted me to have the letters. Why wouldn't Clint just give them to me? I had always disliked him and felt the feeling was mutual, but now I hated him with a vengeance. I couldn't shake off the feeling that he enjoyed making my life a living hell by taking from me the one thing that really mattered to me—a physical memory of my mother.

I spent a few more minutes outside, fighting to clear the fog of anger inside my brain. When it didn't work, I returned to the apartment. Jude appeared in the door the instant I walked in.

"What happened?" she asked, her voice betraying an edge of worry.

"Just the usual," I muttered, and walked past her into my bedroom, slamming the door behind me, then buried myself under the sheets, praying sleep would come and wash away the anger and pain, and anything related to them.

The inability to grant my own mother's last wish felt like a failure to me. With no husband and time running out, my options were depleted.

I had lost the fight.

Chapter 13

IT MUST HAVE been late afternoon when I awoke to the sound of muffled voices coming from the living room. Assuming Jude was home watching television, I sat up and shielded my eyes from the setting sun coming in through the windows. Thanks to Jude's magic elixir, my headache had settled to a bearable level, and the nausea in the pit of my stomach had disappeared.

Time to face the world.

I took a shower and got dressed in black jeans and an oversized T-shirt, twisting my hair in a loose knot at the nape of my neck, not bothering with makeup.

The voices were gone. Apart from the faint traffic noise, the apartment was silent.

"Jude?" I called.

Nothing stirred.

Maybe she had switched off the television set and left already. I knocked on her door and received no answer. I headed down the hall and was about to pass the living room when I clashed with hard muscles. Strong hands wrapped around my waist, steadying me as I peered up into gray-blue eyes, and my mouth went dry again. Realizing I was an idiot, I jumped a step back to put a few inches of distance between us. But the hall was too narrow for us, his proximity overpowering.

"Sorry, I didn't hear you," Chase said. "Are you okay? Did I hurt you?"

I nodded, then shook my head.

*Make up your mind, Hanson.*

"I'm fine. What are you doing here?" I managed to croak, my eyes scanning the living room. But there was no sign of Jude.

"You wouldn't return my calls." His tone was nonchalant, detached, even, as though he didn't notice just how close we were standing and how fast my heart was beating in my chest, the way his gaze traveled to my neck and the roundness of my half-exposed shoulder, and then down the front of my shirt. My breasts peaked in response, straining against the thin fabric of my bra.

"I popped over to make sure you survived last night's

cruel torture of your body."

I ignored his indirect referral to my drunken state. "Who let you in?"

"Jude did. She instructed me to take care of you until she returns, and that's exactly what I'm doing. I'm following her command."

Of course, she had done it again, the little witch. Trust her to use every little opportunity to play her games.

"So, when will she be back?" I asked casually.

"I have no idea." He leaned against the wall and crossed his arms over his broad chest, regarding me amused. "But I'm ready to bet she'll take her time."

I narrowed my eyes. "She will, won't she?"

His lips twitched and there was a dangerously handsome glint of humor in his eyes. "Here we are. Just the two of us."

*He knows you've been trying to avoid him and likes the fact that he's caught you off-guard.*

And, judging by the ever-growing grin on his face, he was enjoying every minute of just how uncomfortable he was making me feel. Or why else would he point out to me that we were alone for no apparent reason?

I groaned inwardly at the realization that I had no escape route. I had no idea how to ignore his sexy body, which was all I could gawk at. It took every ounce of my willpower to turn away when all I wanted was to stare at the sex god before me and ask why the fuck he smelled so good.

"You look nice." Chase pointed to my shirt before his hand touched my hair. "I like it when you wear your hair up like that."

"It's nothing." I shrugged. "I do it every day."

"It suits you perfectly, Laurie." He smiled, his hand still playing with my hair. His eyes were so deep, it made me blush. "I like it natural."

*God.*

The way he said it, it was as if his words carried a double meaning. Or maybe I wanted them to, because his shirt emphasized his broad shoulders and narrow waist, and my naughty thoughts were all I could think about. He looked so delicious, my mind was already undressing him. Before my eyes I could already see those rock-hard abs that were clearly defined beneath his shirt. I fought the need to graze my fingernails over them and see him quiver from my touch.

"Are you okay?" Chase asked. "You look a bit flushed." His tongue flicked across his lower lip, sending a slow, almost painful pull between my legs.

"I told you, I'm fine," I snapped. "Just tired and hungry, that's all." It took all my might to force myself to walk past him into the kitchen and keep my back turned to him as I grabbed a cookie jar and held it up behind him, offering Chase one.

"Is that all you want to share tonight?"

*Holy bang.*

There it was again—the subtle sexual hint. Or maybe not so subtle. Only I wasn't so sure why he kept dropping them.

"Just the cookies," I said shakily. In spite of my better judgment, I was still hoping that it was just a figment of my imagination. My hands trembled so hard I feared I might drop the jar any second.

Damn my hormones and their weakness for a pretty face.

Damn Chase for not making rejecting him easy on me.

Damn me for not being able to interpret the situation correctly much sooner.

I stopped near the table, afraid to turn and look at him. In the silence, I could sense him stepping behind me. And then he leaned forward, his hot breath grazing the delicate skin on my neck until I felt I might just be about to melt.

"Is that all I'll get?" he whispered. His voice was low and husky, betraying a hint of arousal.

My heart jumped into my throat. There was no doubt now.

He was going for it.

*Big time.*

"I heard you the first time, and I think I gave you a

pretty clear response," I whispered, and turned around slowly. He was standing too close, oblivious to the effect he had on me. Or maybe he knew, and it was exactly what he wanted? Our eyes connected, and in an instant he closed the space between us, his hard body pressing into mine as his hands went around my waist, pulling me against his hard muscles.

"You know I want you, Laurie. There's no secret about that," he whispered.

*And he knows you want him. Or else he wouldn't touch you.*

His gaze moved downward to my mouth, settling on it hungrily. I swallowed hard, barely able to breathe. If he kissed me now, I wouldn't resist. The thought hit me with such force that I almost flinched.

I knew I had to get my wits back. Only, I didn't want them back. All I wanted was to run my hands through his hair and pull his mouth onto mine the way I had never done with anybody else before—and all for a good reason. Chase had to stay out of this. It was for his own good. The people in my life weren't safe. Pulling him into the mess that was my life without giving him a choice wasn't fair.

"I know you want me, too, Laurie," he whispered. His hand cupped the back of my neck, and his lips inched just a little bit closer, his breath caressing my mouth. "What's stopping you?"

I couldn't reply. Every fiber of my body wanted him,

but getting what I wanted wasn't an option.

"Why are you holding back?" he insisted.

"I can't," I whispered, prying my gaze off him. "As much as I want to, I can't. I'm sorry."

"That's a shame. You're a challenge. I'll have a great time figuring you out. But damn, you're shy." He leaned in to tuck a strand of hair behind my ear. Ever so slowly, he trailed his fingers down my naked skin to my shoulder.

Shy? He couldn't be serious.

"God, woman." He let out a sharp breath. "Put something on before I forget what my mother taught me and ravish you on the spot."

"What?" I laughed. Where did that come from? My clothes weren't particularly revealing. Besides, it was hot outside. What the heck was I supposed to wear? A ski suit?

"I'm not the kind of man who imposes." He looked at me with way too much intensity. "You'll have to ask for it, because I'm not going to force myself on you."

He smiled and winked as he grabbed the cookie jar out of my hands and plopped down on a chair, biting heartily into a chocolate chip cookie. "Now, that's a cookie I like."

I stared at him. What was that supposed to mean? That he liked me? I wasn't sure. Nor was I sure whether he had actually meant the cookie or me.

"What was that?" I sat down and turned to regard him, my heart beating frantically in my chest. Jude's words about relationships rang in my ears, and my doubts that he wanted me slowly dissipated into thin air. In the soft light of the setting sun, he looked more stunning than ever. And that was the problem. I couldn't be attracted to him.

"Make whatever you want of it." Chase shot me a sexy smile and finished his cookie. "All your decision. As far as I see it, you're single, I'm single. I like you. You like me." He shrugged. He put the jar on the table and leaned forward. "You do the math."

I looked at him, struck speechless. He was still smiling, but his expression had turned into one of bewilderment. Only too late did I realize that he was watching my reaction.

"Yes, I like you, Laurie. Why is that so hard to believe?" He cocked his head to the side, his eyes narrowing at me with a sudden interest. After a small pause, he said, "Tell me. Have you ever been with a man?"

*Oh, lord!*

I turned my eyes away from him to hide the shame in them. There was nothing I could possibly say. Nothing I could explain to him. He sat down next to me, and his hand gripped my chin, forcing me to look at him.

"There's no reason for you to be ashamed, Laurie. Just tell me the truth." He regarded me with a warm expression in his eyes. "If you don't want me to date you, I understand, but I'll need a reason."

He thought I had a choice. I inhaled a sharp breath and

let it out slowly.

"You don't understand," I began, my mood plummeting to new depths.

"I do, actually. I get it. After everything you told me yesterday, I understand you more than ever. You're shy, and you need more time. I just need you to say it."

I looked at him in dismay. Why the heck did he keep talking in riddles?

"Oh, my God," I whispered when the penny finally dropped.

The fact that he thought I lacked sexual experience was the big deal here, but he was way off the mark.

I had literally *no* experience.

I got up, but Chase grabbed my hand to stop me from walking away, and pushed me back down.

"It's not a problem for me, Laurie," he said, all cocky confidence. Of *course* it wasn't a problem for *him*. "I didn't want to tell you, but I want us to be honest with each other. So, I'll make the first step."

"What did you not want to tell me?" I whispered as my mind conjured hundreds of possible scenarios. That he was married. Engaged. Played for the other team. Wanted me sexually, but wasn't interested in more. Strangely, that possibility upset me the most.

His hands settled on the side of my thighs, just above the knees. His light touch built a strange contrast to the determination in his eyes.

"Yesterday, when you were—" He paused, carefully selecting his words.

"Drunk," I prompted.

"Yeah, that." I expected amusement to cross his face, but his expression remained strangely pensive. "I left you in the car with Jude to say goodbye to Clint and Shannon when your stepfather pulled me aside for a chat." He scowled, as though the recollection wasn't a pleasant one.

Suddenly, my pulse quickened, and fear whipped through me. Clint and I didn't exactly have a loving father-daughter relationship. We weren't even friends and had nothing in common, but all those years we had gotten along more or less amiably because I had made sure to keep out of his way. He couldn't have told Chase the truth. Not without consulting me first. Or could he?

"What did he say?" I asked, warily.

"Not much. Like you, he'd had a few glasses too many and was rather cryptic. But he did something else that didn't make sense to me." His scowl deepened as he regarded me intently, probably watching my reaction to what he was about to say. "Like I said, I want us to be honest with each other."

"What did he do?" My voice came out shrill as blood rushed in my ears.

He hesitated. "He offered me money to break off our

engagement."

## Chapter 14

I STARED AT Chase as his words slowly sank in. Clint had offered him money to leave me without knowing that Chase and I weren't really engaged. We weren't even together. In spite of our differences, I had always thought that Clint and I had a silent agreement. That he wanted me to find happiness and the closure I had waited for, while I kept silent about the past. I expected him not to meddle in my affairs just as much as I wanted him to move on and leave me alone.

"Why would he do that?" Chase asked.

I shook my head, signaling that I didn't know. And, truth be told, I didn't know. The entire situation shocked me just as much.

"Are you sure that's what he said? Maybe he offered to *help* with money, or—" I stood up and began pacing the kitchen up and down, my thoughts a maze of confusion and hurt. But in my heart I knew the truth, even though I had yet to admit it.

"There's a lot you haven't told me." It wasn't a question; it was a statement. He was spot-on.

"I can't," I whispered.

Chase moved behind me, and his strong hands settled on my upper arms with enough pressure to force me to turn around. I raised my gaze to meet his. The gentleness I found in his eyes destroyed my last reserve.

"I know it's hard, but I'm here to help." His arms wrapped around me, pulling me against his chest. I buried my face in his shirt and took deep, calming breaths to help me control the tears gathering behind my closed eyelids.

I couldn't cry.

I hadn't cried in years. With my walls up, the tears were long depleted—or so I had thought. But now the walls were coming down, shaking me to the core.

"Please don't ask me to," I whispered weakly.

"But I want to help you," Chase said. "Let me help you, Laurie. I see how much this pains you."

"You don't know what you're getting yourself into." My voice came so low that I doubted he had heard me. For a few moments he remained silent, confirming my thought.

Then he lifted my chin to meet his gaze, and I noticed the stubborn expression in his eyes.

"I want to get involved in whatever you're involved in." His words took me by surprise. "I want you to trust me. Even if it's hard to believe it, I want you to know that you're no longer alone. I'm going to help you."

"But you don't even know what it involves."

"Doesn't matter. All I see is that you're hurting. You're scared."

I laughed darkly. Scared was an understatement. I was freaked out. There was so much panic inside me that it made me wish I could just run—far away. If it weren't for Chase's hands holding me, I might just have.

"I can see that this man has hurt you, Laurie. Don't even try to pretend it's not true."

A tear rolled down my cheek. I wiped it away, angry at myself, angry at Clint for pushing me into such a situation, angry at Chase for not running away when he should have been.

"Why do you want to help me, Chase?" I asked, ignoring his previous statement.

"Because you're special." A soft smile played on his lips. "I really like you, Laurie."

"But you don't know me," I said, unable to hide the anger in my voice. "You know nothing about me." I yanked myself out of his embrace and was turning to leave when his hand grasped my arm, keeping me pinned to the spot.

"Then let me get to know you," he whispered. "The real you."

I snorted. "Trust me. I'm a horrible person. You don't want to know me."

"Leave that to my judgment." His voice was hard. "Even though we're not together, I'm still your fiancé. And to your stepfather: fuck him. I'm staying. That's what I said to him, you know?"

My heart lurched as I stared at him in dismay.

"Money can't buy me." He regarded me, his gaze hard again. "I chose this job because I wanted to. Not because I had to. And now I want to help you."

He wanted to stay. He wanted to know. He stuck with me even though he didn't have to. Only God knew how much money Clint had offered him. Money I didn't have.

I struggled to choose between the conflicting thoughts in my head. In the end, I found myself nodding, defeated.

"Fine," I said sharply. "I'll tell you what I can, and then you can make up your mind whether you want to do this. You can decide what to think of it."

*What you think of me.*

"I won't change my mind." His hand cupped my face. "Whatever it is, thanks for trusting me."

I shrugged in indifference, even though his soft expression rattled me to the core. It wasn't a matter of trust;

it was a ploy to push him away.

"We should sit down. Then I'll tell you." I was ready to reveal the parts that made sense. The parts Jude knew. The parts that were ready to be unveiled. Everything else I'd keep in the dark, the way I liked it to stay. No questions asked.

*Chapter 15*

ONCE I BEGAN to speak, the words just gushed out with no regard as to who was listening. It was as though a rivulet of emotions had given way to a river bursting the dam that had acted as its walls. I kept my head low, my gaze avoiding the man sitting beside me, listening in silence as I told the story I had kept buried inside for years.

"I never knew my father, only that he was someone very important and rich. So when he died shortly after I was born, my grandparents insisted my mother remarry because they didn't want to see me growing up without a father," I began. "She married Clint when I was about eight, and shortly after we were playing happy family." I shrugged, sensing Chase's unspoken question from the way he seemed to tense up. "I didn't mind. Because I had never met my father, it was nice to have someone around. Someone who asked about school and pretended to care about what I was wearing. And then I was sent to a private school, and we didn't really spend a lot of time as a family, except for the festive holidays." I looked up and smiled.

Chase smiled weakly, but remained quiet which, I figured, was my clue to continue. "It was shortly after my ninth birthday that things started to change. It was a hot August day when my mother became really sick. Around that time Clint took over her business affairs. As time went by, she got worse and started to be gone for weeks at a time. Sometimes Clint took me to visit her in those hospitals. They looked more like rest homes with bars on the windows and nurses watching her day and night." I looked up into Chase's frown. "Only later, as I grew older, did I understand that it was a mental health institution. Eventually, Clint explained that she had suffered a nervous breakdown and as such had to be treated, but the treatment wasn't really working."

"She was being treated for a mental breakdown?" The incredulity in Chase's voice didn't escape me. At some point he had leaned forward, elbows resting on his thighs, as though he was eager to hear the story but didn't want to press too hard. I moistened my lips, unsure whether he'd think me crazy if I told him the rest, even though I wanted to...badly.

I nodded. "I guess he wasn't really telling me the truth...or the extent of her mental problems. Maybe he thought it'd be too hard for me to accept what was happening to my mom. What girl wants to acknowledge that her mom is sick in the head while all her friends go shopping with their mothers and have a great time?"

The images began to take shape in my mind—grim pictures painted in sadness and despair, in the colors of a child's ignorance and her inability to grasp the bigger meaning.

"I remember her coming home one day," I whispered, lost in reminiscence. "She seemed fragile, horribly thin, but she was so much better. She laughed a lot and wanted to spend time with me. She kept making promises, that we'd do some gardening together, which she'd never done before. And that we'd grow wild rose bushes around the fence, which was absurd because she wasn't into gardening or any sort of outdoor activity. It was like she was a completely different person, but I didn't think anything of it. All that mattered to me was that she was back and seemed healthy. I was so thankful that she wanted to spend time with me. And then the weird things started to happen." I looked up into Chase's face. His eyes were hooded by dark lashes, but there was a glint of pensiveness in them.

A soft shudder ran down my spine, and for a moment I was pushed back into the body of a child, watching my mother's frail figure from the huge bay windows in the living room.

"What weird things?" Chase asked softly.

I shook my head, hesitating, as I let the memories invade me until my throat felt tight and my hands started shaking.

"She began to lock herself in her room, always flinching at every sound. She freaked so much she kept sending me out of the house to keep me away because I made her nervous." I paused as I allowed the picture of me, as a ten-year-old sitting on the lawn, gazing up at the dark windows and wondering when she'd let me in, to cloud my vision. It was such a bleak memory that I flinched and instantly pushed it to the back of my mind.

"I don't know why she was so afraid," I continued. "But she always tried to hide her fear, as though she didn't want to burden me with it. A few times I crept back into the house to watch her from the staircase. She was always standing in front of the window in her bedroom, surveying the driveway for hours until Clint came home from work, and then she'd get dressed and join us for dinner, like she hadn't been this nervous mess all day long." I shuddered. "It was eerie watching her turn from one person into another just like that. I became afraid. Not for me, but for her. I feared that she'd fall back into her mental health problems. And she did eventually."

"Do you think that"—Chase paused, considering his words—"Clint might have hurt her?"

"I don't think so." I shook my head, even though the possibility had crossed my mind countless times. "I mean, not that I know of. I saw her getting dressed. She had no bruises on her body, if that's what you're referring to. She just seemed crazy, always talking to herself."

"Did you ever talk to Clint about her mental problems?"

"No."

"Why not?" Chase asked.

"Because I thought he knew. I mean, it was he who insisted she get professional help. How could he not know? They were married. They slept in the same bedroom, for God's sake. Her nails were always bitten to their pulp, and her gaze was that of a crazy person. But even if I wanted to talk, Clint was always busy. Sometimes he didn't come home for days and could barely be reached on his phone. I couldn't talk to someone who had turned into a stranger again." I fell silent again as I fought the feelings of guilt bubbling to the surface.

The guilt of knowing too much. Of not having done anything—when I should have. For many years, I had blamed myself, wishing I had talked to someone about the change. But it had come gradually, sneaking up on her like a venomous snake, until, one day, it was too late.

"It took me years, but now I understand why Clint sent her to get professional help," I began slowly, and opened my fist. The tissue between my fingers was crumpled, reflecting the state I was in. "One evening, when she couldn't reach Clint, I found her in the garden, crying. She was holding a pregnancy stick in her hands, so I asked whether I was going to have a brother or sister." My mood darkened as I thought back to that fateful day. "I had never seen her so furious in my entire life. I had seen many shades of hers, but never anything like it. Her eyes were burning with rage. She was just—"

I broke off, struggling for words, but Chase didn't pressure me. Instead, his gaze lingered on me patiently, waiting for me to resume my narration when I felt ready for it.

"I'm sad to say, but it was in that moment that I thought she should never have left the institution," I said weakly.

Chase's hand around mine anchored me in the present so I wouldn't get lost in the past I had often relived it in my thoughts.

"Did she hurt you?" he asked softly.

"No, that's not it. She never did." My voice was weak, almost childlike. "But that day she was erratic. Crazy. She started to smash things and talk nonsense, like that the devil was coming to get her and her baby, and she held a shard of glass to her neck, threatening to kill herself." I took a deep breath. "I think she was scared and that fear somehow changed her. Anyway, she made me swear that I wouldn't tell anyone about the baby, and I didn't. But"—I looked up into Chase's eyes and found him listening intently—"I found the pregnancy stick later in the trash. It showed that she wasn't actually pregnant. It was just her imagination. I think not telling Clint about the imaginary baby was a mistake." I drew a sharp breath. "If I had told him, he could have helped her. A few days later, when I thought things had calmed down, she committed suicide while he was away. The police said she had poisoned herself, and all her clothes were found scattered in her bedroom, like she had raided her closet."

Chase opened his mouth to speak when I held up my hand, stopping him. I didn't want to hear that he was sorry, because that wasn't what I wanted to hear. Everything had happened such a long time ago that all the wounds had long since healed. What had remained, though, was a mystery I could never solve.

"There's a reason I'm telling you this, Chase," I whispered gravely. "Something else has been bothering me. It's haunted me all the years, and I think it's the reason why Clint offered you money."

Unable to stay still for a moment longer, I got up from the sofa and walked over to the window, keeping my back turned to Chase. This was the one thing I had never shared with anyone.

The air grew silent, and all I could hear were the cars outside.

"The morning of the day she disappeared, I was late for school, but she wasn't in a hurry to let me go," I began. "She pulled me aside and told me that she was sorry. That I shouldn't be angry with her for what she had done, but she was worried for my safety. That I must never go after the money, but that I should try to get my hands on the letters because they would explain everything."

"What letters?" Chase asked.

"The letters in her will. The only thing she left me," I explained. "By committing suicide, she left everything to Clint. The mansion. All her money. Everything she had received from her father—my grandfather."

I turned around to face him. His eyes were narrowed as he processed my words.

Eventually he said, "That's...strange."

He had meant to say something other than "strange." I could see it in his expression, but I didn't press the issue.

"I guess." There was a hard tone in my voice. I sounded bitter, I realized, but I couldn't help myself. Too many years had passed, and yet they did nothing to reduce the pain of her leaving me to face the world alone.

"Did you read them?" Chase asked, filling the silence.

"The letters?" I shook my head, signaling that I hadn't. "That's why I needed you."

"I'm sorry. I'm afraid I don't follow."

I clasped my hands together. "My mother specifically asked that I be married before my twenty-third birthday in order to get the letters," I said.

He drew a long breath. "And your twenty-third birthday is—"

"In twenty days."

"Ah." His eyes widened just a little bit. "In twenty days? But you're not married. You're just engaged."

"Pretend-engaged." I rolled my eyes at Chase, stating the obvious. "I don't even know why I can't just forget all about them and move on. There's probably nothing important in them anyway, just a madwoman's senseless rambling."

"But she was your mother," Chase said. "And those letters are the only thing she left you."

I nodded gravely. Maybe he didn't know what I was feeling, but he certainly knew why those letters meant so much to me.

"That's true. But she was still crazy. And they're probably just stupid letters," I said, repeating the one thing I had kept telling myself over and over again for the past few years. Lies to myself to get over the fact that she hadn't loved me enough to stay alive and see me grow up and do all the things mothers did with their daughters.

"They're not stupid letters, Laurie." His fingers stroked my face, pressing gently until I looked up to meet his determined gaze. "You said she was scared, maybe not just for you, but for herself as well. Maybe she knew something, and that's why she cut you out of the will."

"Or maybe she was crazy as bat shit." I laughed darkly.

"No," Chase said, his gaze never leaving me. "Clint offering me money to get rid of me? That only proves he has something to hide. What if there was something really important in those letters?"

I stared at him, at the way his eyes seemed to shimmer with intelligence.

"I'll admit it crossed my mind, but I always thought…." I left the rest unfinished.

"What?" He frowned at me.

"My stepfather gave her the medication. I always thought she was quite lucid…until she took the pills he gave her. But maybe I was imagining things. I was just a child. Maybe I'm crazy thinking all this."

When I remained quiet, he continued. "You're not crazy, Laurie. You actually might be on to something." He pulled me to him, and for a moment I thought—feared— he'd kiss me. But the kiss never came. "That's why you need me. And I'd be happy to help you."

My heart skipped a beat or two.

Why did I like the sound of that so much? And why did I like it even more coming from this stranger's beautiful mouth?

For a moment we just stared at each other, the silence heavy between us.

"You know what?" he asked. "I think we should get married."

"What?" I gaped at him, unsure whether I had heard right.

Chase shrugged and pulled away, his face turned so I couldn't see his expression.

"I mean it. We're both single, with no commitments. It would solve all your problems. What's the harm?"

"What's the harm?" I laughed.

He turned back to me, and in that instant I caught the glimmer in his eyes.

*Determination.*

Whatever Clint had said and done had only persuaded Chase to want to help me.

"This is about the worst proposal I've ever head of," I said jokingly.

"That's because it's an indecent proposal," Chase said. "You pay me to help you and in return you let me date you, with all its implications." He paused, letting me get the hint. Which I did, loud and clear. "We get married, you get the letters. And if you're not into dating, no harm done. I make some money, and that sounds fair to me."

I eyed him carefully, but his expression remained nonchalant. Unreadable. "You realize we might have to stay married for a while, right?"

"Let's give it a year."

"That's a long time." I stared at him, waiting for a sign that it was nothing but a joke.

"Doesn't have to be." He grinned with mischief, but his eyes remained solemn, the glint in them intense. "What matters is that you get what's yours."

"You don't understand, Chase," I whispered. "My mom was crazy. There's a chance that the letters might not be worth anything."

He shrugged. "That's a risk we'll take."

"I'm not sure it's a good idea," I mumbled.

"Laurie." He touched my shoulder. "You owe it to your mom to try to get those letters. She wanted you to have them. If marrying is what it takes, then so be it."

"It's a good plan and it would work, but"—I paused, unsure how to put it—"I don't have the money to pay you for your services. I'm not rich. I'm not the heiress to anything. I wasn't included in her will. I haven't even figured out how to keep myself afloat with the mounting bills trudging in on a daily basis. Even if I wanted to do this, I couldn't possibly pay you, Chase," I whispered. "I don't have the money, and I doubt I'll have it in a year. I can barely afford to pay my rent."

Chase nodded. "I know, Laurie. And I'm not doing it for the money, which his why I offered you Option A," he said, his hand touching mine gently. "I don't need it, meaning you can repay me whenever you feel like it in any form you want. All that matters is that you get some answers."

Now, that sparked my curiosity.

*When something sounds too good to be true, it probably is....* The saying rang in the back of my mind.

"If it's not about money, why would you make such an offer, then?" I asked. "You don't know me. We've just met. There are plenty of other girls you can date."

"I just want to help because—" He shrugged again.

"Because?"

He hesitated for a second as he gathered his thoughts.

"I like you, Laurie. I already said that. And I have a feeling that you need those letters, not just because you deserve them." He looked at me with kindness. "I don't think it's right that your stepfather has control over your life. The letters could help you turn your life around, maybe even help you understand what was going on with your mom."

He was right. Too right.

I took a sharp breath and kept it trapped in my lungs until they began to burn from the strain. Only as the pain became unpleasant did I exhale. Just as he knew there was more to me than I had let on, I knew there was more to Chase than met the eye. We didn't know each other, but, for inexplicable reason, I wanted to trust him. For once in my life, I didn't want to be disappointed. However, the nagging feeling that I would owe him the rest of my life was too big. As if sensing my distress, Chase pulled me to him.

"Laurie," he whispered. "I want to be here for you."

"After everything I told you, you still want in?" I looked up, my heart jumping so hard I was sure he'd hear it. His hands trailed down my waist and settled on my butt. Without a warning, he pulled me close against him until I could feel his breath on my lips. Beneath his clothes, I felt the hardness of his muscles and the strength emanating from him.

"Sure. No questions asked." His eyes were like deep, dark pools as he leaned forward just a little bit more and his gaze settled on my mouth. For a second, we just stood there, caught in the moment, frozen in time. My heart skipped a beat as realization dawned. He was going to kiss me. And I wanted him to—more than ever.

His mouth came crashing down on mine—probing, savoring, sending a shivery rush between my legs. With a soft moan, I parted my lips and let his tongue invade the cave of my mouth. I could taste cookies, chocolate, coffee, and *him*—the perfect recipe to send me into a drunken state from which I didn't want to emerge. A flame flickered to life within my core, and twinges of electricity pulsed through my private parts, urging me to take whatever he had to offer. If one kiss could do this to me, I wondered what would happen if I asked for more.

I pressed my hungry body against him and felt the heat of his skin beneath his clothes. He was already hard, his erection brushing my abdomen, and for the first time in my life I didn't feel the need to run away. I wanted to touch him. Feel him. Expose him to my gaze.

Chase pried his lips off mine, leaving me breathless and slightly disoriented as he put some distance between us. "I'm going to marry you, Laurie, but under one condition," he whispered, his flushed face mirroring the way I felt. "I want to take you out on a date. A real date."

Chapter 16

CHASE HAD BEEN adamant that if we were to marry, we at least make it look real. Given that I didn't exactly have an array of other choices, I agreed, and we arranged a first date when Chase expressed his first condition. He insisted that I dressed accordingly, or, in his words, "Wear something nice."

I had guessed he meant something elegant, maybe made from a flowing fabric. Naturally, a chiffon dress was my first choice as I ascended the stairs of our apartment building.

Chase was leaning against his expensive car, his eyes sweeping over my legs appreciatively as his lips curled into a wicked smile.

"Hi," I said shyly, my gaze appraising his black slacks and light blue shirt that seemed to match the color of his eyes. He was so beautiful I almost choked on my breath, my mind unable to grasp the fact that in less than half an hour, I'd be having dinner with the most beautiful man I had ever seen. I felt like a fan who was about to meet her Hollywood crush for the first time. He wasn't just making me nervous; his presence seemed to highlight and magnify my inexperience to glaring proportions.

"You look stunning," Chase said, sweeping me into his arms to kiss my cheek.

My throat constricted, and my brain switched off. As his lips touched my skin, I wanted to say something clever— something a mature woman with plenty of experience would say—only, the words remained glued to the back of my throat.

Chase pried his arms off me, and we were in the car. A strong wind rustled through the open windows and blew a few strands of my hair into my face. I was hurrying to brush them aside when I realized Chase had started the engine and now was staring at my naked legs.

"What?" I turned to regard him and narrowed my eyes as I took in the amused smile on his lips. "Don't you like what I'm wearing?"

"Of course I do." He shook his head and met my gaze—and something sparkled in his eyes. "Anything shorter, and I would have insisted we head up to your place and order in."

My heart thumped. "Why?"

He let out a small laugh. "You know why, Laurie. I doubt I would have been able to kept my hands off you, and making out in a restaurant isn't something you'd be comfortable with."

He wanted to make out.

I bit my lip hard to suppress a smile, but the heat scorching my face probably betrayed my true feelings. Ever since we had kissed, a rose hue and a smile had remained etched on my face. He was pure eye candy, flirty and easy to converse with. Even though a relationship would never happen, at least I could enjoy the moment.

"I have to say you're really...." I struggled for words.

"Awesome?"

"Persistent, stubborn. Maybe even bordering on insufferable." I smiled at him. "Tell me, do you ever give up when a woman says no?"

"I don't, Laurie." He put the car in gear. "I would never give up because I always get what I want. Then again, I never had to chase. You're the first one to cause me both blue balls and wet dreams."

"I don't believe you," I whispered, shocked at his boldness.

"Why would I lie to you?" He killed the engine, and

then he turned to me, his eyes full of mischief and something else. My breath caught in my throat as he leaned forward, and I was bracing myself for his kiss when his fingers brushed my leg gingerly, lingering for a second or two, before he picked up something from the floor. "You lost your journal."

I stared at the light pink journal, confused, the meaning of his words not really hitting home. It wasn't the only thing I had lost. Under his touch, I felt like I was losing every inch of my self-control...or ability to think.

"Oh." I had been so busy staring at Chase, I hadn't realized my bag had opened and the contents had spilled onto the seat and floor. As he handed me the light pink journal, my fingers brushed his, and an electric spark traveled down my arm.

"Thanks," I muttered, my voice alien in my ears.

"You're welcome." His eyes rested on me for an awkward moment.

"Shouldn't we get going?" I said when his strange gaze became too uncomfortable.

"Sure." He started the engine and pulled out of the parking space. The car roared, and we sped through the busy L.A. streets. Never in my life had I felt this way: this absurd longing to kiss Chase again whenever he was sitting next to me, his hand gracing mine accidentally as he changed lanes. We'd only driven for a few minutes before he pulled over.

"Are you ready? We're here." Without waiting for my answer, Chase opened his door and jumped out. I slung my handbag over my shoulder and let him help me out of the car. I was about to head for a quaint little Italian café advertising the best pizza in town when Chase's fingers curled around my elbow.

"What are you doing?"

I turned to take in the amused glint in his eyes. "You promised dinner."

"Yes." He nodded slowly. "But not in there." He pointed to the large building on the other side of the street. "That's where we're headed."

"The Lux?" I stared at one of the most overpriced places in L.A. "You can't just walk in there without a reservation." I didn't want to point out that the place was booked months in advance.

"I wasn't going to." He intertwined his fingers with mine and pulled me after him through the stagnant traffic. "Guess what? I have an old friend who works here. He got us a nice table."

"Oh." I hurried my pace to keep up with him, almost oblivious to the luxury cars and—was that an A-list movie star ascending the stairs, disappearing behind the doors? "Are you sure about this?"

The place looked way out of my league, not least

because I couldn't afford it.

"Relax, Laurie," he whispered in my ear. "Just go with it."

"But—" I opened my mouth to let out a string of protests, but the words remained stuck in my throat. "Why here?" was all I managed to say.

"What's wrong with taking my future wife to one of the best restaurants in L.A.?"

*Everything.*

I just stared at his profile, at a loss for words.

"I've heard they specialize in candlelight dinners." Chase winked and held the door open.

I mumbled a grim "thank you" and walked in, struck speechless yet again. This wasn't supposed to happen to me. All my life I had lived in fear. I had been running for so long, I had stopped believing that something like this would ever take place. Sure, I had read about it in books, seen it in movies, heard about it from gushing friends, but I had always been convinced that romance wasn't real.

Chase was slowly starting to prove me wrong.

Chapter 17

THE LUX WAS located in a top 4,000-square-foot space, complete with cushioned booths and fascinating greenery. It was a place where celebrities hung out and, as such, was always fully booked for months in advance. That Chase had a friend who worked here was unfathomable but nothing I'd consider unbelievable, considering the fact that, as an actor, he probably knew a few famous people.

A maître d' led us past several booths, each one decorated with flower bouquets and white candles, and stopped in front of the most beautiful one overlooking a water fountain behind a glass wall. Soft music played in the background. The love seats looked comfortable and inviting. The whole atmosphere was so serene I could have spent hours in here, ready to forget Clint and the real world.

"You like it?" Chase took the seat opposite from me and rested his hands on the white tablecloth, watching me.

"Like? Try love it," I gushed. "It looks so expensive, I'm surprised you don't have to pay just for sitting and swallowing the air."

Chase laughed—the sound caressing my nerve endings and reverberating through my body. It was so beautiful, I wished it would never subside.

"You should try the food. It's delicious...just like you." He handed me the menu and waited for the waiter to fill our glasses with water.

"Have you ever been here before?" I asked, ignoring the sudden cartwheel my heart did.

"Yes." He smiled. "But never with a woman as beautiful as you."

"Yeah, right." I smirked. "Aren't you the charmer?"

"In my line of job, I have to be, but with you it comes naturally."

He was laying on the charm...and boy, did it work when it shouldn't have. I stared at him, at the way he cocked his head whenever he looked at me, and realized I had to keep a strong hold on my heart if I didn't want to fall for him and his gray-blue eyes.

I put the menu down and cleared my throat. "Why are you doing this, Chase?" I paused, considering my words.

"You could have picked a less lavish place, and yet here we are."

He shrugged. "Why would I do that when I didn't want to? You're only getting married once."

*Oh, come on!*

"I know, but…." The tip of my tongue flicked over my lip as I carefully prepared my words. "This wouldn't be your usual marriage, Chase. It's all about convenience. We don't have a real relationship."

"Yet." The word cut through the air and made me flinch. My heart jumped into my mouth as the meaning of it sank in.

"We will never have a real relationship," I whispered so low I wasn't sure he could hear me. "You don't know me, and I don't know you. You don't know what a relationship with me could mean for you."

"I'm a patient man. I'm not asking you now." His fingers brushed my hand over the table. "You never know what tomorrow brings. All I'm asking is that you give us a chance to get to know each other, to figure out whether there could be more between us."

I frowned. "What exactly?"

"That you'll have to figure out yourself."

Pretending I didn't hear, I swallowed hard and pulled my hand out of his grip to pick up the menu. There was nothing between us. Period. Maybe just a bit of mutual understanding. Okay, a tiny bit of attraction. But that was it, and I wanted it to stay that way.

We both scanned the menu in silence.

"I'm having today's three-menu course. Chicken tagine with figs and olives sounds too good to resist. What do you think, Laurie?" Chase's voice drew me back from my shock at the prices as the list progressed, each one more absurd than the last.

*Holy shit.*

Why hadn't he told me in advance we'd be visiting this place so I could have taken out a loan?

A thousand bucks for a piece of special truffle cake? Even the salad cost more than an entire evening plus leftovers for the next day at the place where Jude and I usually ate on special occasions. This was ridiculous. I had to settle for a salad. I could do that, couldn't I?

"I don't know." I scanned the list once more to find the cheapest item...and found nothing that even remotely fit into my financial plan. "I'm not really that hungry."

Which was a lie. I was starving. The air smelled mouth-wateringly delicious, and my stomach had growled ever since a waiter had passed us by with a tray full of what looked like green pasta and salmon.

"There must be something you like, Laurie." Did I detect a hint of irritation in his voice?

I sighed and scanned the menu one last time, my gaze

glued to the prices as though my mind could make them shrink.

"I'll go with the French garlic soup," I said at last, my voice thin. Closing the menu, I caught Chase's grim expression and remembered that garlic wasn't so great for kissing. He probably figured the same, and he had expressed an interest in making out later, so...I changed my mind. "Or maybe the mussel soup."

I groaned inwardly. Assuming that we'd be ending the night with a kiss was ridiculous. Where the hell did that come from? Not that I didn't want to, but I hadn't been so obvious about it, had I?

"Soup?" Chase sounded incredulous, almost pissed. "I'm paying for dinner, Laurie, and I insist you choose something that's actually nourishing." He tapped his fingers on the menu. I didn't want to point out that soup *was* nourishing. People all over the world ate it. "Unless you're on a diet?" He raised his eyebrow, but it wasn't with amusement, and I remembered our first date slash interview, during which he had expressed distaste for women who couldn't tuck into a wholesome helping of spare ribs.

"Okay, if you insist, I'll have the same. Chicken tagine with figs and olives, it is." I sighed. "Can we at least split the bill?" His scowl lifted almost instantly.

"Not going to happen." He looked at me, amused. "But

194

I'm taking you up on your offer."

I frowned. "What offer?"

He grinned. "After this date, when I drop you off at your home, I expect another kiss."

I stared at him, unsure whether I should laugh off his absurd demand or pretend I didn't hear him. In the end, I decided to go with the second option.

"I hardly know anything about you," I said to both brush him off and steer the conversation in a different direction.

A waiter approached with our wine glasses. I folded the napkin as he lit some candles and then retreated again.

"There isn't much to know," Chase said as soon as we were alone again.

He appeared to be a mystery, and he wanted to keep it that way. But just because I could see that much didn't mean it pleased me.

"Look." I sighed. "I'm not really the dating type. Even if I wanted to do this, the whole marriage thing, I couldn't possibly pay you, Chase," I whispered. "I don't have the money, and I doubt I'll have it in a year. I can barely afford to pay my rent."

"We can agree on installments."

I grimaced.

"I was just joking," Chase said, taking a sip of his wine. "I told you, it's not about the money."

*Everything's about something in life. There's no such thing as a free ride.*

The knowledge had been burning inside my head for the past few hours, lingering in my brain like a disease.

Sure, I knew he wanted to date, but it couldn't be the only thing he wanted.

"There has to be something in it for you," I said slowly, rolling the wine glass between my hands. "People don't do good deeds out of goodwill."

"I do. I want to help. Your pussy would be a great bonus, though." He grinned, and for a moment I wasn't sure whether he was indeed joking.

I shook my head at his unwillingness to share his true feelings with me. Much like the fire in the candles burning, it had a life on its own. I was too tired to deal with a hot, walking enigma.

"If you had led the life I have, you'd do the same." His voice drew my attention back to him.

I raised my brows. "How so?"

"We aren't so different, Laurie. Maybe if I tell you something about me, you'll understand why I'm doing this."

My breath hitched. He was *finally* ready to disclose more about his life...and yet I couldn't push it.

"You don't have to. It's fine." Even though I wanted to know more about his past, I didn't like the gravity in his voice. His expression had turned serious, his eyes betraying something I couldn't identify, and seeing him like that hurt me in a way I didn't understand.

Our gazes locked, and I almost flinched at the dark glint in his beautiful gray-blue eyes. Hurt. Disappointed. He had a haunted look, the kind of look people get when they experience great trauma and loss.

"No, it's okay. I want to. You told me something about you, and I want to do the same." He paused for a moment and moistened his lips. The sudden distant look in his eyes betrayed that he was traveling into a past long gone. "My mother died on the road when I was nine. We were all traveling together that night. I remember I was sleeping when someone shouted, waking me up. I was disoriented, and I remember having a strange feeling, like I could tell something bad was about happen." He drew a sharp breath and let it out slowly. "It happened so fast. One minute I was sleeping, and the next, our bus crashed into a tree on the side of the road. My mother couldn't be helped in time. There was nothing anyone could do."

"I'm so sorry," I whispered.

He nodded. "It was hard. But it was even harder growing up and finding that, at some point, my memory became fuzzy. I just couldn't remember her." He took another sip, his glance far away in the past. "I never really knew much about her, anyway, and she left me nothing of importance. The pictures I have of her might just as well be of a stranger." He looked up to me, his eyes focusing on me with renewed interest. "At least your mom has left you something. I like the idea that she left you personal letters, even if they turn out to be nothing but drivel. They're still from her, and I want you to have them. Is that so hard to understand?"

"That's selfless," I said, meaning it.

"Maybe," Chase said, hesitating. "It just feels right. Like I'm solving a puzzle from my own past through you. But I'm also doing it because, well, you have no one else. There aren't many days left, Laurie. If I'm not marrying you, who else could possibly help you but me? Try walking away from this situation. It's not as easy as you make it sound."

I remained silent as I considered his words. It was true. I didn't have much time left. Besides, the chance of coming across someone else who'd agree to help me was like finding a needle in a haystack. But Chase felt as though he couldn't walk away. My guilty conscience kicked in.

"I appreciate it, but I don't want to cause you any trouble," I whispered.

"You're not. And, to be honest, I'm kind of enjoying this." His mouth twitched into a hesitant smile as he continued, and I sensed that the conversation was about to take yet another turn. "If we're doing this, then we'll have to agree on some ground rules."

I raised my brows. "Like?"

"Like no dating or sleeping with others."

"I thought you weren't the commitment type."

"I'm not," Chase said, his smile still in place. "But I take care of my health and needs. Seeing that we'll be dating, I only want to ensure that whatever we'll be doing we'll only do with each other. And there's a lot I'll be teaching you."

*Oh, god.*

I looked away before he could glimpse the major blush scorching my cheeks.

"What makes you think I'll sleep with you?" I asked, barely able to control the sudden tremor in my voice.

He bent forward, and his hand closed around mine. "Isn't that what you've been wanting ever since setting your eyes on me?"

Was that a question or a statement?

Still avoiding his gaze, I bit my lip hard until I thought I might just draw blood.

"No. Of course not."

He laughed at my unconvincing attempt to disguise the truth.

"There's nothing wrong about wanting someone, Laurie," he whispered, and his thumb began to circle the sensitive skin on my hand.

*Oh, for crying out loud.*

Did he *have* to be so full of himself?

"I need to use the restroom." Without waiting for his

answer, I jumped up, ready to dash for the exit, when his reply came.

"You can run away from me all you want now. Soon enough, you'll be heading in the opposite direction, and I'll be there."

That stopped me in mid-stride. Slowly, I turned around to face him, my blood boiling in my veins. It began to boil even hotter when I met the naughty glimpse in his eyes, which were the color of storm clouds and hurricanes.

"What makes you so sure about that?"

"I see it in your eyes, Laurie." He got up and closed the space between us.

Ready to sweep me off my feet.

Ready to drown me in the lust I was beginning to feel for his hard body.

Luckily, our booth was shielded from prying eyes.

"You'll have to get used to your needs," he whispered. "If you don't listen to your body, your passion will make you unhappy, and I can't afford that."

"Maybe I want you just a little bit," I said through gritted teeth. "But you can't force me to give in."

"I would never impose myself on you," Chase said, his hard voice matching mine in determination. "You'll be the one begging me for more."

I laughed, but the tone sounded fake and choked. "I doubt that."

His sexy lips curled up into a gorgeous smile. "Well, that's because you haven't had me inside you…yet."

The sudden heat between my legs almost immobilized me. Holding my head up high, I stormed for the bathroom and slammed the door behind me, unsure whether I was angry with myself for hiding my attraction to him so badly, or with Chase for being so brutally honest and ungentlemanly about it.

In the end, I decided to be angry with Jude for bringing him into my life. It was easier to hide behind a wall of pretense-anger than to admit that I had never felt so intrigued in my entire life.

Chapter 18

THE MOON SHIMMERED against the black night sky, bathing the street in a silvery stream. As we exited the restaurant, Chase's arm was wrapped around me, and he pulled me to him possessively. We walked down the stairs, huddled close together, my head spinning from so much good food, alcohol...and Chase's intoxicating presence.

The visit to the restroom had helped me gain my composure, after which I even managed to have a drink. Chase acted as if nothing had happened, and then we ordered dinner and engaged in small talk—nothing too heavy. As it turned out, we shared many interests and hobbies. I tried hard to listen when he talked about his taste in music, but my mind kept swaying back to his last words

and the possibility of us getting intimate, and I found myself wondering what would happen and what it would mean for me.

I didn't know what made me think that, but there was something interesting about him. Maybe not interesting so much as intriguing, as if his mere presence stirred me deep inside, awakening parts of me I never knew existed.

"One day I'll take you to see them live in concert. What do you think?" Chase said as we reached his car.

See whom in concert?

My attention snapped back to him, and I realized I had no idea what he was talking about.

"Laurie?" Chase prompted, his hand lingering on the passenger door, one or two inches from my hip. The way he regarded me made me painfully aware of just how close we were standing and how easy it would have been to tangle my fingers in his hair and invite him to take charge.

"What's so great about them?" I moistened my suddenly parched lips as my brain fought to remember our train of conversation.

"You have to listen to them live. Just pure awesomeness." His fingertips brushed my hip as he opened the door while his other hand touched the small of my back to guide me inside. It was such a small, innocent movement, and yet I found myself more perturbed than ever.

"Chase—" My voice came hoarse and heavy.

*What, Laurie?*

Ask him to touch me again? Ask him to stop being so damn sexy and do all those innocent things that shouldn't have made me feel the way they did? I couldn't say any of that. Not now. Not ever.

"Yes?" His gaze was interested and sharp, as if he'd sensed the change in me.

I was shaking my head grimly when I noticed a flash. Instinctively, my eyes scanned the parked cars on the other side of the road, just as another flash caught my attention. Given that the Lux was frequented by celebrities, I wasn't surprised to see a paparazzo with a long-lens camera glued to his face...only it was focused on us. I turned back the other way to see if someone might be standing behind us, but no one was there.

"That's strange," Chase whispered. His tone sent a chill through me.

"What?" I asked, even though I knew already what was wrong. I spun slowly, my gaze searching for the long-lens camera. And then I saw him again, focused on us, snapping away. It was such a strange moment. The knowledge of being watched felt surreal. It made me feel powerless, as though I was in a bad dream and unable to wake up.

Chase was an actor. Maybe the guy had recognized him, and Chase wasn't the small-time artist he pretended to be. I should have headed over and just asked, but my feet

remained glued to the spot. It was so easy to pretend that Chase was the object of attention that I almost believed it.

But only almost.

A grain of fear settled in my heart and instantly began to grow. When the photographer noticed my lingering stare, he hastily pulled out of the parking lot and sped past us.

"Did you see him?" I whispered in shock, and regarded Chase's features. His expression was a mixture of anger and disbelief. There was no question he had seen the guy.

"What the fuck?" he muttered. "Get in, Laurie."

Without waiting for my reply, he ushered me into the car and rounded it. For a few seconds, we sat in silence, my blood pumping hard through my veins, our giddy excitement replaced with tension.

"Are you okay?" Chase's voice drew me back. He was back to his usual composed self.

I nodded silently, even though I wasn't sure it was the truth. "Is this always happening to you? Because if it is, it's scary as hell." I laughed in an awkward attempt to infuse some humor into the situation but, judging by Chase's expression, failed miserably.

His jaw set, and his eyes turned a shade darker. "I'll take you home." He pushed the key into the ignition, fingers hovering, ready to turn.

"Don't." My voice sounded a little too shrill as my hand clasped around his forearm, stopping him. A frown crossed his face, and the vein in his neck began to pulse slightly. His eyes assessed me with sudden worry.

"Please don't take me home just yet," I whispered, and bit my lip, unsure how to put the sudden waves of fear into words. It was such an irrational reaction, and yet I couldn't help myself. "He was there."

"Who?"

"The same guy who just took pictures of us. Or at least I think it was him." My voice quivered, and I cleared my throat to steady it. "A few days ago, Jude saw someone standing in front of our window. She thought she saw a flash, like that of a camera." Chase gave me a questioning look, and I continued. "I watched him take several pictures of *us*, Chase." I scanned the dark street outside the car window out of fear he might have returned, but the guy was gone. I almost expected Chase to laugh and call me silly, maybe even stupid, but he didn't.

"I don't like this." Chase started the engine and hit the accelerator.

"Where are we going?" I asked. "I can't go home."

"You're not going home," he said. "I'm taking you to my place. You can stay as long as you want."

I leaned my forehead against the cold glass. Thousands of reasons as to why someone would want to take pictures of me began to swirl in my head, but none of them sounded plausible. We remained silent throughout the drive to downtown L.A., but I could feel Chase's worried glance on me from time to time.

Eventually, we arrived at his place, which turned out to be a penthouse in a tall building with a glass front. Chase parked the car in an underground garage, and we rode up the elevator. The flashing red lights of several security cameras should have infused a sense of safety into me, but didn't. As he unlocked the door, I peered hastily over my shoulder, as though to ensure no one had followed us, which was ridiculous, given the fact that the building had a 24/7 security guard on duty and a concierge manned the front desk, and the cameras probably filmed every corner.

"Come in." Chase held the door open and then closed it behind us, hiding us from prying eyes. A shaky breath escaped my lips as I shrugged out of my jacket and handed it to Chase, who stacked it away in a wardrobe compartment hidden in the wall.

In spite of my trembling fingers, the fog of fear inside my mind slowly began to lift, and I found myself itching for a chance to take in the place. Chase's most intimate things were here, and I was standing just a few feet away.

"Can I get you some water? A drink?" Chase asked, and motioned me to enter the living room.

"Do you have any wine?" I let my gaze sweep over the spiral staircase in the middle of the room, the dramatic furnishings, and the stunning panoramic view of the city lights. I had never seen L.A. from this height, and had a hard time not gawking.

"Yeah, I don't think it's a good idea to—" Chase said, regarding me.

I cut him off. "Don't tell me if or how much I can drink. It's not your business, Chase." Usually, I didn't drink. But the pressure of having to get married was slowly getting to me, and I felt as though there was no other option but to stay sedated to numb my brain and the unease in the pit of my stomach.

"Okay." He looked unconvinced. I feared he'd try to change my mind, but he didn't. "Your choice. I'll be back in one minute."

I watched him leave and then turned back to the window, suddenly transported to a different time, when luxury had been a part of my life and I was too young to realize that not everyone lived in a mansion with hardwood floors, shiny candelabras, and silverware that was polished daily. Absent-mindedly, I brushed my fingers over the marble fireplace and took in the elegant living area kept in warm wooden tones. It was so different from anything I had ever seen. So like *him*—full of warmth and mystery.

*Chase was rich.*

The realization hit me like a bomb. Maybe a different, more modern kind of rich than the old-family money I had been born into, but rich, nonetheless. His lavish lifestyle was probably the result of hard work and talent, no doubt, but it didn't make me feel more comfortable around it. I had sensed it all along, but I just didn't realize *how* rich.

"Your place is beautiful," I said when he returned with two glasses and set them down on a glass coffee table. "The view is second to none."

"I suppose." He motioned to the cream leather couch overlooking the fireplace and slumped down with a sigh. I followed his unspoken request and sat down, tucking my legs beneath me. The leather felt warm and soft beneath my fingers.

*Expensive.*

I swallowed hard as my mood plummeted to a new low.

"Will you report it?" Chase asked, oblivious to the tumult inside me.

"And tell them what?" I laughed. "I have no proof of anything, don't know who the guy was, have no idea what he wants, or why he was taking pictures." I brushed my hair out of my eyes. "The thing is, I don't even know whether it wasn't just a coincidence."

*I tend to overreact a lot.*

"You're right." He nodded and handed me a glass of wine. "It's probably nothing, Laurie. But if there is, if he so much as crosses your path again, I'll kick the living shit out of him."

"Thanks." I smiled weakly. Even though I knew Chase

didn't mean any of it, his words infused a sense of safety and confidence into me. I took a sip or two of wine and leaned back, slowly relaxing.

"Do you have an ex who might be spying on you?" Chase asked.

"No." I shook my head, frowning. "That guy wasn't an ex."

"Maybe someone who might hire a private detective rather than do the work himself."

I shook my head again. He wasn't getting it. The idea was absurd because there *was* no ex, at least not someone who had been close enough to me to call him that.

"Then we have every reason to assume it's your stepfather," Chase said. His grave tone sent a shiver down my spine. I peered from him to the untouched glass and then back up at him.

"Clint?" I asked, incredulously. "You think he's capable of doing it?" Even as I asked the question, I knew the answer.

Chase shrugged. "If someone offers you money to break off his stepdaughter's engagement, then why not add spying to the list? There's a reason why he doesn't want our marriage preparations to proceed."

My gaze fell on my glass. The liquid looked as thick and dark red as blood. "Money," I whispered as I recalled the contract.

"Money? Maybe." He sounded doubtful. "Although I'd say he has enough of it. As far as you told me, you never tried to get your share of your family's wealth. Money's hardly a motivating factor."

I took another sip and looked up, my gaze imploring him to understand.

"Chase," I began. "I haven't told you everything. If I marry you, not only do I get the letters, but also half of Waterfront Shore."

"But you said your mom—"

"She left everything to Clint," I cut him off. "However, my grandfather left only half of the house to her, who was supposed to act as my guardian until I turned twenty-three. After her death, he never had the chance to change his will, because he died four weeks later. Her last will hadn't even been read yet. It's a huge house worth millions, meaning I'd either have to move back home and live with Clint, or he'd be forced to sell and share the profits or"—I took a sharp breath and let it out slowly—"he'd have to pay me out of his pocket."

I let the words linger in the air.

"That's the reason why he and Shannon keep pushing for me to move back in," I continued after a pause. "I agreed to pass my share on to him as long as I get the letters. But obviously, he's scared my future husband might try to change my mind, so he offered me a quarter of the money the mansion's worth *now* as long as I sign a contract that I won't want more later. If I accept the money, I won't ever have any future claim. But I don't want anything, not now, nor later."

"My God, Laurie. Why would you refuse what should be yours?" Chase looked perplexed. "It should all be yours. Not his."

I should have seen the question coming. Anyone with half a brain would ask it, but even if I explained, no one would understand. Chase hadn't seen what I had seen, hadn't carried the burden of so much wealth on his shoulders.

"I have my reasons," I whispered. "Just accept it."

His expression changed from confusion to disbelief. He opened his mouth, as though to say something, then closed it again.

"It's…complicated," I added. "Like I told you, my mom was scared, and I trust her judgment. Long story short, I will never take that money."

Chase remained silent, his eyes focused on me as he seemed to process my words. Strangely, I felt guilty, and I had no idea why.

"So, what are you thinking?" I asked when I could no longer stand the silence.

"That your grandfather died very soon after your mother's death."

I nodded. "Yeah, he died before he could change his will to leave the entire estate to me."

"I don't like this," he said. "After everything you told me, I'm more convinced than ever that you're not safe from Clint."

Even though the thought was ridiculous, I couldn't help the pang of fear settling like a rock in my stomach. "What makes you say that?"

"I don't know. Call it intuition or whatever, but people don't just try to pay others off." His glance hardened, and filled with determination and anger. "I don't trust him."

I smiled weakly. "Now you sound like me. I don't want you to get involved. I don't know what the deal is with Clint or what his plans are, but I don't want you to get hurt."

"Don't worry about me. I can take care of myself." His hands wrapped around mine, and something passed between us—something dark and heavy. My heart fluttered a bit faster, but not because of my blatant attraction to him. I trusted Chase, I really did, but for some reason I couldn't shake off the feeling that there was more to him than met the eye.

"I know you do, but—"

"Laurie." His sharp tone cut me off. "He's trying to stop you. If marrying you is what it takes to get those letters and reveal the truth, then so be it. I'll marry you, even if I have to drag you down that aisle myself and force that ring on your finger."

It was a joke; I could tell that much from the amused glint in his eyes.

"You won't let the bastard control your life," he continued, more seriously.

Clint wasn't. I had made sure of that a long time ago.

I leaned my face against Chase's chest. For a while, I focused on my senses: hearing his soft, slightly ragged breath, smelling wafts of his masculine aftershave, and feeling the touch of his warm hands on my back.

"I wish there was something I could do for you, too. I don't like owing you," I said eventually.

"Actually, I have a thought—"

He didn't have to say it. I knew *exactly* what he wanted. I cut him short by pressing my mouth against his, and our lips connected in a quick, hot kiss.

He pushed me back softly to regard me with eyes that seemed to burn. "Laurie." His voice came hoarse, and a small laugh escaped his lips. "I wasn't talking about a kiss, which is great, don't get me wrong, and more than I bargained for, but—" He paused, hesitating.

"What?"

"I don't want you to think you owe me for something I want to do for you. I don't want to take. I want to give."

I raised my eyebrows, an amused smile on my lips. "So what did you want from me, then?"

"Nothing that matters now." He smiled and stood, pulling me up with him. "Come on. Let me give you a grand tour of my place."

Chapter 19

CHASE SHOWED ME around his place and told me repeatedly that I was welcome to stay as long as I wanted. Eventually, his words had the desired effect, and I began to feel safe. It was a little after midnight when I stepped out of the shower and wrapped a fluffy towel around my naked body.

"Thanks for letting me stay. I hope it's not too much trouble for you and your girlfriend," I said, standing in the doorway and eyeing the leather couch, which was now covered with pillows and a bedspread. Wearing clean clothes—a long T-shirt and boxer shorts Chase had lent me for the night—and with my teeth brushed with his spare brush, I felt composed and was back to my usual self again.

"Sure. And I don't have a girlfriend, Laurie. I think I established that already, but I appreciate the thought." Chase tucked his hands into the pockets of his jeans as his eyes scanned my naked legs. "You look nice."

"Oh, please." I could feel the telltale signs of an oncoming blush and wished I could stop my body from giving me away every time Chase said something that got to me.

"I mean it." He grinned and stepped in front of me to brush a wet strand of hair behind my ear. "Wearing my clothes suits you. You know what was in those shorts? Now they're brushing your skin. It's almost like *I'm* touching you…down there."

My jaw dropped. Talk about mortifyingly frank. I should have bolted out the door. Slapped him. Anything but…smile like an idiot and think about what his fingers would feel like…down there.

His face inched closer, and his hot breath grazed my ear. "It's such a shame you don't see how beautiful you are."

*Whoa.*

I inhaled a shaky breath and put some distance between us before he took the next step in whatever plan he was pursuing.

"Maybe I don't want to." I shrugged as nonchalantly as I could and settled on the sofa, covering my legs with a blanket as I changed the subject. "Most people get so superficial and materialistic, they forget what life is all about."

"That might be true," he said. "But sometimes people are stuck in a state of stagnation, not living or expanding their potential. They forget that both their soul and their body have needs."

"What are you saying?" I bit my lip and regarded him intently.

"Whatever you want to make of it. My words are always open to interpretation." He gave me a mysterious smile and then winked at me to follow. I remained seated.

"So you think I'm not reaching my full potential." It wasn't a question; it was a statement lined with pure, sweet venom. I tried my *best* to be my best self. I always explored possibilities and opportunities. Having a man tell me otherwise made my blood boil.

"I said no such thing." He drew a long breath and let it out slowly. I narrowed my eyes at him, waiting, wondering. People were criticizing me all the time and I didn't give a monkey's ass about it, so why was it so hard to take coming from him?

"You did." I raised my chin defiantly. "And I very much beg to differ. Whatever you think I'm not doing with my life, it's a *choice*."

He nodded slowly, his eyes fixed on the floor. For a moment, we avoided each other's gaze, the tension palpable in the air. And then Chase reached me in two long strides and cupped my face between his hands, forcing me to look him into those impossibly strange eyes.

"You're scared of intimacy. I get it. But that doesn't make me want to fuck you less. That's all I'll say." And with that he let go of me and turned around, calling over his shoulder, "Are you coming?"

My mouth went dry, and all the blood drained from my face.

*Coming where?* I felt like asking, but the words remained stuck in my throat in a blubbering mess. I followed him into his lavish bedroom with its beautiful dark damask wallpaper and crystal lamps on either side of the bed. My gaze instantly focused on the bed covered with silk sheets the color of chocolate and countless pillows. I swallowed hard, unsure whether to proceed. This felt intimate. Too intimate. Even from where I stood, I could smell that the sheets had been changed recently, as though in preparation for a female visitor.

"I made your room ready," Chase said, and pointed at the bed, which managed to make the entire situation even more awkward.

*Your room?*

When the meaning of his words finally dawned on me, I stared at him in surprise. "Where are *you* sleeping?"

"Outside. On the couch. Sleep tight."

Made sense, given the pillows and blanket on the couch. "I thought I'd sleep there."

He walked past me, clutching a pillow under his arm. "You're my guest, Laurie." With a last glance, he closed the door behind him, leaving me standing in the middle of the room, struck speechless.

"Good night," I murmured too late.

My gaze remained glued to the closed door as I fought a sudden wave of disappointment.

*That's it?*

No good night kiss? Nothing?

I sat down on the soft sheets and peered around me. On the left side was a walk-in closet next to a sitting chair and reading lamp. The floor-to-ceiling windows on the far right provided a beautiful view of the city. The entire atmosphere screamed luxury and comfort. Chase's king-sized bed was so huge, I felt as though I might just be swallowed up whole and I'd be fine with it. With a delighted sigh, I leaned back, spreading my arms out in the process, when my gaze fell on my reflection in the huge sunburst mirror above the bed. My mouth dropped open.

*Holy shit.*

He had a mirror…above his head.

Who had something like that?

People who liked to look at themselves while doing all sorts of dirty things. I felt disgusted, and yet, at the same time, a delicious tremor worked its way through my abdomen and settled between my legs.

I was staring at my pale face in disbelief when a soft knock carried over from the door. My face flushed with heat, as though I had just been caught doing something I wasn't supposed to do.

I rose up on my elbows and called out, "Yeah?"

"Sorry." Chase's head popped in. "I forgot to ask. Do you need anything? Spare pillow? A blanket? A nightcap? Or do you want me to turn on the heat?"

"We're in California." I smiled at him, unable to push the thoughts of Chase's naked reflection in the mirror out of my head.

"Some women freeze. Or so I've heard."

"What about some company?" My heart began to race as I patted the empty space beside me with a confidence I didn't really have.

"You sure?" He sounded surprised, but he didn't decline my offer straight away.

What the heck *was* I doing? Now I couldn't take it back without him thinking I was one of those indecisive women who couldn't make up their minds.

"I can't really let you sleep on that couch in your own apartment." Shoot, now it sounded like an invitation to share my bed, when I had only wanted him to keep me company for a few minutes. I cringed inwardly. At the rate I was going, I'd be buried in my own hole before I knew it.

"I don't really mind." He stepped closer, but still didn't take me up on the invitation.

Didn't mind what? Coming in? Sleeping on the couch?

"I'm serious," I heard myself saying. Talk about trying not to sway him. *Oh, god.* "You've been so nice to me and the couch looks like a medieval rack. I bet it's very expensive and not particularly comfortable and your bed's huge. And soft. We could pile up pillows right in the middle and—" I stopped and bit my lip, wondering why the words kept flowing.

Actually, the sofa didn't look so bad. Surely he knew I didn't really mean my brainless invitation, and that I was just being friendly.

"Okay."

*What?*

All heat drained from my face, but Chase was already out the door to get God knows what.

Within two minutes he was back and his jeans and shirt were gone. My mouth went dry at the glimpse of bronze skin and hard muscles. He liked to work out—a lot—which wasn't surprising considering his profession. But did he have to look *so* good?

I flicked my tongue over my lips nervously, wondering how the heck I could possibly sleep next to *him* and not think of what his body might feel like under my exploring fingers.

"Is that what you're wearing to bed?" I brushed my hair out of my eyes and pointed to the boxers and his snug, white shirt. He arranged the pillows in the middle of the bed until they had formed a little wall, his gaze avoiding mine.

"No." His lips twitched. "I usually sleep naked."

"Oh, okay." I snorted, uneasy. "Yeah, that's not going to happen, Chase."

*Damn.*

He wasn't even in bed yet and already the temperature had risen a few degrees.

"Don't worry, I *can* keep them on." His tone was meant to instill confidence in me, but only made me more nervous, maybe because he hadn't said that he *would* keep them on.

He patted the makeshift wall, which looked like it would crumble if one of us so much as turned in our sleep. "Is this working for you?"

Nodding, I didn't dare glance at him, at his strong legs, or the muscles flexed in his arms. The mattress dipped beneath his weight. From the corner of my eye, I saw him prop up on one elbow, regarding me.

"What?" I turned sharply, unsure what the heck he was waiting for, and noticed the glint of amusement in his eyes.

"You're sleeping on my side. The light switch...it's next

to you." He pointed to the bedside table, and the glint of amusement flashed again.

I followed his line of vision to what resembled a small water bottle made of stainless steel pinned to the wall. It was the most obscure light switch I had ever seen—not that I had seen many. Confused, my fingers brushed over the smooth surface. Now, how could I switch off the damn thing? There was no button to press. No cord to pull, and most certainly no switch. Nothing to give away how this thing worked. I brushed my fingers up and down, this time in slow motion, and Chase let out a low chuckle. That's when I realized the thing looked a bit phallic and the motion of my fingers was bound to attract naughty thoughts—at least in my dirty imagination.

As though burned, I quickly pulled my hand away. "How do you—" My voice broke in mid-sentence when he leaned over me, his strong arm carelessly draping over my heaving chest, like it belonged there.

And then the room was bathed in darkness with only the moonlight streaming through the open drapes and the city lights twinkling in the black sky.

As my eyes adjusted, I could make out Chase's features, his gray-blue eyes two dark spots that seemed to shimmer with mystery. Suddenly aware of his all-consuming presence, I held my breath as I wondered what he was thinking. Ever so slowly he leaned forward and his mouth conquered mine. My breath swished out of me in a guttural moan. I ran my fingers through his hair and pulled him just a little bit closer to me, my mouth opening to welcome his hot tongue. But his kiss remained soft and gentle against my lips, my mind frozen in the moment, as if time had stopped.

In the silence of the night, his mouth against mine felt different. It was intoxicating, powerful, and inexorable. Tiny jolts of electricity rushed through my abdomen, settling in that one little spot no one had ever touched.

I pressed my breasts against him and my nipples beaded instantly at contact, as though the darkness around us was a gate and all I had needed was a kiss to open my body for him.

Running my hands down his back, I bit his lower lip and he rewarded me with an appreciative moan that caressed my senses. Touching him was intoxicating, terrifying, but also addictive. I couldn't take it while at the same time I wanted more...whatever the consequences.

My tongue flicked past his lips and into his mouth. It was just a little bit, but enough to break through the gates of his self-control. I gasped when he sucked my lower lip into his mouth and dipped his tongue into my willing mouth while his hands began to roam over my body to remove my clothes, stroking, pinching, sending waves of pleasure through me.

"Chase." My breath hitched in my throat, his name

trapped on my lips and stifled by his exploring tongue.

At some point he shifted on top of me and his knee parted my legs, the cold air grazing my most sensitive spot. His hardness pressed against my thigh, fascinating me, urging me to touch it.

For a moment I considered reaching down to stroke him just to know what it'd feel like, but Chase was faster, more decisive in his actions.

His hands moved lower, stroking my body with a passion no water or wind could control. My heartbeat raced with fear and anticipation as my foggy mind fought to make a decision whether to stop him right there and then. Or allow him to go just a little further to find out what I had been wondering ever since we met. I wanted to know what touching and intimate kissing meant. I wanted to feel certain parts of his body buried deep inside me, pinning me to the bed the way I imagined every time I so much as heard his name, his tongue in my mouth, rendering me unable to speak.

"God, Laurie." A labored breath escaped his lips. I laughed because it pleased me to see he wasn't so unaffected.

"More," I whispered, meaning it. I had no idea what *more* would entail, but I was ready to let him decide, even if he wanted to go all the way, even if I was nothing but a conquest to him.

His mouth trailed down to my breasts, latching onto one hard nipple, and he tugged at it gentle, sucking and licking in equal measures. I arched my back involuntarily, asking for more. He shifted his attention to the other nipple before trailing further down, past my stomach, lower and lower.

I held my breath when he started placing soft butterfly kisses on my inner thigh.

"What are you doing?" I whispered and tried to push my legs together, but his hands forced my knees wide apart, my flaming sex inches from his lips. Pushing up on my elbows, I regarded him in the darkness. His expression was unreadable, his grip hard on my skin, probably leaving a bruise or two in the process. I felt so hot and powerless all I could do was stare at him as our eyes connected.

"Isn't it obvious?" He planted another soft kiss on my thigh while rubbing the beginning of a stubble against my sensitive skin.

What the hell was I doing? My sex clenched, and not in a bad way.

"I can't give you what you want, Chase," I whispered, mortified at the fact that he was settled between my legs and I could smell the scent of our arousal in the air.

"I know you're a virgin." He tilted his head up, his eyes locking with mine. His lips parted in a slow, delicious kiss.

*A notch in his bedpost.*

I shook my head, unwilling to believe what I knew to be

the truth.

How do you know that I'm a virgin? I wanted to ask, but my lips remained glued together as he planted another kiss on my inner thigh. "I don't mind your lack of sexual experience. I find it enticing. In fact, I'd love to be your teacher. I promise I won't ever hurt you as long as you trust me enough when I push your boundaries."

What the heck?

Those weren't the words of your usual guy. How much experience did *he* have and what did he mean by 'boundaries?'

"Chase, I think this isn't—"

A good idea? Damn right it wasn't. It was the most stupid, careless move I had ever made. So why couldn't I just say it? I swallowed and tried again, "I'm not ready. I can't sleep with you."

And never would.

"Relax," came his reply before he lowered his mouth between my thighs. His hot breath hit my clit a moment before his tongue began to circle it in slow motion. My heart slammed hard against my ribcage and waves of pleasure fired through me. In my mind, I knew I had to be strong, but strong was the word to describe my ever-growing lust.

Chase's grip around my thigh's tightened, keeping my legs parted. I couldn't have clenched them shut even if I wanted to.

"I said relax, Laurie. I'm not going to do something you'll regret," he whispered, his voice almost forceful. "Beside me fucking you, there are other ways to make you come. Other ways that don't involve anything of mine inside you, though I must admit it's a tempting thought. But, like I said, I'm a patient man. I can wait until one day you'll ask me for it."

I stared at him. "I won't ask."

He let out a deep throaty laugh. "Life is full of surprises. You never know where pleasure takes you, or how far you would go to get more of it." His fingers moved between my legs in soft circles, sending delightful shivers through my body.

I wanted to ask what he meant. I wanted to draw my conversation away from topics that involved intimacy or sex—do anything to keep my mind busy, but somehow…nothing mattered anymore.

I didn't want to feel anything, and yet my traitorous body began to respond to his touch. My breathing came heavy as his breath caressed my skin and his tongue brushed the thin fabric of my panties, the motion almost unravelling me.

Before I realized what was happening, his hand tugged my panties aside, exposing my soft flesh. I whimpered when the cold air hit my sex. And then I realized it wasn't the air but his breath on me—inhaling my scent.

I had to put a stop to this before things spiraled out of control. The knowledge was there, but my body didn't move to follow my brain's command. All it wanted was Chase's lips on my skin, doing things to me that no other man had done before.

"Don't," I whispered so low I wasn't sure the words came out of my mouth. Chase ignored me. He flicked a finger over my clit, once, twice, and then replaced it with soft short kisses, each one sweeter than the others.

Sucking in my shaky breath, I gazed into the mirror on the ceiling to regard Chase's dark shadow between my legs. He seemed focused to the point of total oblivion, unaware of the hurricane of emotions spinning inside me.

I gasped when his tongue began to swirl in slow patters while his hand roamed over my inner thighs, sending a cluster of electric currents through me that felt so delicious I almost wanted to—

*No.*

I shook my head to clear the haze settling within my mind. I couldn't surrender control. And yet his tongue made me gasp involuntarily at the delicious sensations threatening to rock my core.

Intense.

Intoxicating.

"You like this, Laurie?" Chase's hoarse voice was barely

a whisper, but the lust within it couldn't be more obvious.

*Like this?*

How could I not?

I bit my lip hard until the want became almost unbearable, and peeled my gaze off the sexy image in the mirror as a deep moan fought its way past my lips.

"That's it, baby," Chase whispered approvingly. "I want you hot and bothered. By the time I'm done with you, you'll be panting my name."

Hell, yeah, I had no doubt about that.

His lips were so close on my soft flesh, threatening to break my willpower, and yet not close enough. I let out another stifled moan and dug my fingernails into his soft pillows to stop me from unraveling beneath his touch, my innermost being ready to crumble, my body willing to do things I never thought I would do.

"Chase," I whispered, my voice begging him to stop or at least to make a mistake so that I could pull away, while at the same time I was hoping he would continue so I could get lost in the fire his talented mouth had created.

He was perfect, I realized. His lips, his movements. A man of experience, I was sure of that. He must have fucked countless women before me, all more experienced and willing to return the pleasure. All ready to give him what he expected of them. While I was eager to touch him, I had no idea how.

"You taste like honey, Laurie," he whispered. "You know that's my favorite kind of sugar?"

Before I could come up with a reply, his thumb brushed my entrance and began to rub teasingly, not entering me.

It already felt so great, I wondered what his hardness inside me would feel like.

His fingers clutched at my thighs, forcing them wide open, while his tongue continued to lap at my soft flesh, the tip entering me, then pulling out in a dramatic move to continue licking my clit. My hands grasped at the pillows for support and I bit my lip hard, as the flame in my womb began to spread. My core clenched in desperate need to be filled and stretched.

"Chase," I said, my raspy tone alien in my ears. "I don't think I can control myself."

"Do you want me to enter you?" The question was soft, and harmless, the tone conversational, as though he was asking whether I wanted a glass of water. "Remember, you have to ask for it." His fingers rubbed against my entrance again, spreading my wetness.

"Yes," I whispered. "Please."

"There is a 'please?'" he asked, amused. "Never saw that one coming."

Frowning, I bit my tongue. I would have loved to get up and see that irritating smile of his wiped off his face, but the truth was…'please' had just become my favorite word. I

232

wanted him so much I feared he had become a necessity. I opened my mouth to speak, but his lips were back on my clit, teasing me, and then his finger was probing my entry again. Soft, playful, as if he wanted to test me, but had no intention to enter. His tongue flicked over my clit with such a precision and speed that I had to close my eyes to stop the spinning.

Oh, fuck that.

He was going to tease me hard.

"I want your finger inside me." In a moment of lust-induced madness, the words flew past my lips before I could stop them. My cheeks instantly burned. Thank God that it was dark and he couldn't see the telltale sign of mortification on my face.

Before I had a chance to brace himself, his finger found his way inside me in one slow thrust, the friction almost pushing me off the edge.

"Jesus. You're tight, Laurie," Chase whispered, pulling his finger out only to pin my hips down on the silk pillow, cupping my ass as he brought my core closer to his talented mouth.

"Can you do something for me and just relax?" he asked, his hot breath caressing my sensitive skin.

Too weak to answer, I nodded, even though I had no idea how people *could* relax in such a situation. It wasn't so much fear of him, but of breaking my own promise to never sleep with a man. And yet my treacherous clit twitched—as if it was already bewitched, asking to have what I had never had before.

His tongue started to swirl again, and his lips suckled at my sensitive clit. A raging firestorm whipped inside me, making me tremble with lust, threatening to stifle the thoughts in my mind, while forcing my body to do strange things, like lifting my hips to his willing tongue and pushing his finger deeper inside me.

Oh, God, I wanted him so bad and it was painfully clear. He was the kind of mistake I wanted to make, but a mistake nonetheless. Even though the knowledge lingered in my mind, I couldn't act on it.

Chase, I realized, was a suitable name, given the situation. I had been chasing after this moment, both wanting and fearing it, only to get caught in the momentum of it all. Never before had I felt such longing and desperation that I was ready to do whatever it took to have *him*—if only for a few minutes. As if sensing the inner chaos inside me, he slipped the entire length of his finger into me, the chafing sensation making me gasp with enjoyment, before he pulled out again.

"No, don't stop," I whispered, barely audible.

*Oh, God.*

What was he doing with me? To me?

The thrusts of his finger became excruciating and a

slow, burning tug began to fill me. My legs trembled. A wet sensation gathered between my legs as Chase continued to impale me, driving deep inside me as if he owned me. Heat rushed within me, and something else…some I had read about so often, and yet never really understood.

My fingers fisted in the sheets beneath me, and a moan escaped my mouth as he pulled out his finger, only to replace it with two. I arched my back and lifted my hips ever so slightly. If he continued his torture, I'd explode. I opened my mouth to ask for more, when he propped up on one elbow, and leaned over me. His mouth closed on mine, and while his fingers continued to thrust inside me, his thumb found my clit. My head began to spin. If from kissing or from the way Chase kept entering me in now slow but measured moves, I had no idea. All I knew was that it wasn't enough. I had to have more.

I pulled him to me, raising my hips in the hope he'd get the message, but he continued his torture.

"Chase, I'm ready," I whispered into his mouth.

There, I had said it. My virginity was about to fly out the window and I couldn't wait for it to happen.

"No, you're not," Chase whispered so low I wasn't sure I had heard him. Following his words with actions, he stopped his delicious torture and pulled his fingers out of me, leaving a feeling of throbbing emptiness behind.

"Why not?" I asked quietly, disappointment and hurt

fighting for the center spot position.

"Because you're not ready yet." Avoiding my stunned gaze, he shrugged.

"I'm wet for you. How does that not make me ready?" I whispered, cringing at my honesty. "And I *really* want to."

Desperately.

"I know. But just because you want me doesn't make you ready."

In the soft light of the moon, I watched him get up and pull the covers over my naked body.

Did I do something wrong? I had no idea and I was too mortified to ask.

"Where are you going?" I asked, sitting up.

"I'm sleeping on the couch."

"But…" My unspoken protest died on my lips.

"I have to." He groaned, though I couldn't tell whether it was with displeasure or something else. "Unless you want me to get wild and take advantage of your body, it's better that I sleep far away from you."

The sofa wasn't exactly far away, I wanted to point out, but didn't. Instead, I tried to read the mixed emotions on his face. I wanted him so badly, my body screamed for his touch, begging me to ask for the kind of release only he could give, but no words passed my lips.

Did I do something wrong?

Had he realized that I was far too inexperienced and was

now thinking that I was a waste of his time?

"Someday I'll take you long and hard, Laurie. Make no mistake about that." He leaned forward until his breath brushed the corners of my mouth, and tucked a strand of hair behind my ear. "But for now I'm going to leave you like this."

"Why?" I croaked.

"Call it payback, baby."

I frowned and opened my mouth to ask what the hell he was talking about when he pressed a long finger against my lips, stopping me in the process. I could smell myself on his skin, almost taste my juices on him.

"Remember our first date?" I nodded and he cocked his head, his lips twitching. "Your no-nonsense business pretense gave me the mother of hard-ons. I had to make myself cum twice to even get you remotely out of my system."

My eyes widened at his blunt statement. The image of a naked Chase groaning in ecstasy entered my head and made my clit pulse to life again.

"Will you be okay?" he asked, probably misinterpreting the heavy silence.

I suppressed the need to roll my eyes.

What was I supposed to answer, without sounding in desperate need of him and whatever he had to offer? I didn't want to give him the satisfaction, but more importantly, I didn't want to admit to myself that Jude had been right all along: I wasn't as immune to Chase's charm as I had pretended to be.

I pulled the sheets up my chest, ignoring the wet sensation covering my folds. "What happened today will never happen again," I muttered at last. The disappointment in my voice rang clear and true.

Chase let out a strangled laugh. "Give me a few more dates, and you'll be the one begging me to fuck you. You were quite close to it today. Like I told you before, I have no doubt about that. As you remember, we still have a whole fake marriage left and I have every intention of making you plead before I give you what you want." His lips touched mine in a fleeting kiss. "Good night, Laurie."

The door closed behind him. For a long time I stared at the empty space, my thoughts a never-ending trail of Chase, images and fragments of conversations.

I should have been angry at his arrogance, but for some inexplicable reason I found myself gripped by panic because Chase was right. He had no idea just how close I had been to begging. When at least half an hour had passed and no sounds came from outside the bedroom, I finally found the courage to open my legs and touch myself, but quickly lost interest, more frustrated than before because it wasn't the same.

My body wanted *him* and only him.

# Chapter 20

I WOKE TO the soft scent of waffles and coffee wafting over from the kitchen. Groaning, I shielded my eyes against the early morning sun. A look at my watch showed it was past 9 a.m. and from the sounds carrying over from the kitchen, Chase was long awake. I jumped out of the bed and then opened the door to secretly make my way down the hall, past the open plan kitchen, to the bathroom, where I had left my clothes the previous night, when Chase spied me.

"Hey, sleepyhead." He smiled and offered me a red coffee mug with the inscription "Boss."

My heart skipped a beat at his sight. His torso was naked, with hard muscles beneath taut bronze skin and the happy trail I had accidentally touched last night on full display.

"I hope you don't mind," Chase said, pointing to his chest as if sensing my thoughts. "It's been too hot in here. Probably the hottest day in California." An amused brow shot up as his gaze traveled from my face to my chest and legs, and then back up again.

A blush covered my cheek as I realized he was talking about the things we did the previous night. My clit twitched at the memory and a soft tug gathered between my legs. Even though his exploring fingers had granted me enough pleasure to last me a lifetime, something inside me asked for a different kind of release.

After Chase had left in the middle of the night, I had stared at the ceiling for hours, my mind going over and over the sensation of his lips on mine, the way he touched me, and the unnatural wetness between my legs. Seeing him standing half-naked in front of me, I could feel myself going wet again.

"Coffee?" Chase asked.

"Please."

He turned his back to me as he filled two cups of steaming black coffee. Sunlight streamed through the windows, emphasizing his strong muscles and taut skin. My eyes scanned his sexy body hungrily and came to rest on his tattoo: a black snake covering half of the left side of his back, its mouth agape. Its tail almost reached all the way around his waist, as if to protect him or maybe to attack.

Chase turned back to me and handed me a cup with steaming black coffee—just the way I like it.

"Thanks." To hide the guilty look on my face, I took a tentative sip and managed to burn my tongue. "How do you know I like my coffee black?" I asked.

He shrugged. "Just a guess. But if you want sugar and cream, I have some."

"I'm fine." I took another sip of my coffee and eyed the two plates with blueberry waffles. "That looks great."

"I made us breakfast." He placed the plates on the table and sat down. "Be my guest."

Realizing how hungry I was, I took a bite and nodded, impressed. "They're really good." I took another bite as my gaze trailed back to his tattoo.

"Did you sleep well?" Chase asked and took a mouthful of his waffles.

"Great, actually. Your bed is pure heaven." It was the truth. His bed was heavenly, but I knew something else had helped me sleep.

I remembered the waves of ecstasy tearing through my abdomen, and the thought drove a pang of heat through my cheeks.

"You're welcome to stay as long as you want," Chase repeated the same words as the night before. Either he really wanted me around or he was just being friendly. As much as I wished I could stay, life was calling. In the darkness of the night, I had been scared and alone. In the safety of the daylight, however, last night's demons were long gone and the whole paparazzo incident felt like a distant memory. I had to get back to my routine, not least because I was beginning to enjoy my time with Chase a little too much.

*Guard your heart.*

"I have to go. Jude's probably worried about me." At his surprised glance, I added weakly, "This is the first time I ever stayed away for the night."

"I'm not so sure about that."

I frowned. "It's the truth. I never spent the night with anyone before."

"That's not what I meant, Laurie." He smiled, but it didn't reach his eyes. "I wanted to say that it's not a good idea to go back to your place now." In spite of his smile, his tone worried me.

"Why not?" I asked slowly.

He grabbed a manila envelope and pushed it into my trembling hands, his facial expression tense. "Have a look." He nodded his head encouragingly, but his expression didn't soften. "It arrived this morning, addressed to me." His eyes met mine, hesitating, heavy with words unspoken. "And you. To *us*."

The strange undertones in his voice sent a chill down my spine.

As I stared at the thick brown envelope, my heart heartbeat picked up in speed. I turned it slowly, prolonging the moment. My mouth dropped open as I finally glimpsed the names and Chase's home address. Why on earth would someone address an envelope to us when we weren't even living together? And worse yet, this wasn't even a real relationship, and I hadn't told anyone about it.

"What's inside?" I peered up at Chase, my fingers lingering over the brown paper, strangely afraid to open it.

*Afraid to reveal the truth.*

Chase looked at me for a few seconds that seemed to stretch into an eternity, and I realized his good mood had been all pretense. He was worried and trying hard to hide it.

My fingers squeezed in at the corners and opened the flap of the envelope. But even before I pulled out the papers, I knew those were long-lens pictures of Chase and me, taken the previous day, as we exited the restaurant.

We looked happy…like a real couple. Laughing. Bodies pressed together to escape the evening chill. It would have been a nice snapshot, were it not for our faces circled with a red marker pen, giving the impression that we were a target.

Was someone *targeting* us?

But why? I had no money. Nothing anyone would want from me.

I shook my head, as though to sort through the thoughts inside my mind.

We had been followed. That in itself was scary as hell. Add a few photographs and the target sign, and I knew I wouldn't be able to walk down the street without peering over my shoulder repeatedly for a long time.

"It's a warning," I whispered in shock as realization dawned on me. "But why would anyone want to send us a warning?"

"I have no idea." Chase drew a sharp breath and his gray-blue eyes hardened into layers of ice. I had never seen anyone look so cold and composed, and for some reason it almost scared me more than the letter.

Maybe I didn't know the man I was about to marry particularly well.

Maybe I didn't know him at all.

I stared at the long lens pictures in my hand. There were six, all of them showing Chase and me, leaving a restaurant hand in hand, then me cocking my head to the side, confused, before looking in the direction of the camera with shock finally registering on my face.

"Why would someone mark us as targets?" I whispered. "It makes no sense."

"I have no idea." Chase drew a sharp breath and shook his head slowly.

"It's a warning," I whispered again, this time with more

confidence.

"Are you sure, Laurie?"

"No, but—" I looked up, taking in the frown line on his usually smooth forehead. "What other explanation is there? The guy watched us yesterday, snapping pictures in the process. It's probably the same guy who was outside my window a few days ago, the day I announced to Clint that I was going to get married." A shiver ran down my spine. "I can only assume that Clint's hired a private detective to spy on us."

I scanned the pictures again, my gaze focusing on the thick red line of the marker, and Chase's name along with mine.

*To*

*Mr. Wright and Miss Hanson.*

As if we were a real couple.

"You really think your stepfather would go this far?" Chase asked. I would have expected a hint of doubt in his voice, but his tone was nonchalant, as if nothing was below Clint.

"Go this far?" I laughed darkly. "I turned down his offer to one quarter of my mother's fortune. He basically has it all. What more could he possibly want?"

"Maybe he thinks he can't trust you."

"I don't want anything from him. I told his attorney loud and clear." I balled my hands to fists as a wave of disbelief and anger tore through me. Clint had many faults—too many to count, which included being a greedy jerk—but spying on me was taking it a bit too far. "Do you realize what this means, Chase?" I looked up into his gray-blue eyes, eager to read his thoughts. His expression remained dark but casual, his thoughts veiled. If he worried, he didn't show it.

"The guy followed us from the restaurant," I continued. "He knows where you live. He knows that I spent the night with you. He's spying on me; he might have done it for months or years, and I didn't notice. He probably knows we're not really dating."

"No." Chase shook his head. "I don't think so."

"What then?" I raised my eyebrows, prompting him to explain.

"Sending you this is a message." He pointed to the manila envelope in my hands. "He's making sure you follow through with your plans for the right reasons."

"He's always tried to control me," I whispered in hate and slammed the envelope back on the table. "He's making my life a living hell." I was so angry, tears stung my eyes.

Chase stepped next to me and grabbed the envelope out of my hands, then placed it on the coffee table. "We're getting married as planned. His private detective can take as many pictures as he wants. Clint won't find out a thing."

"Except that we're not a real couple, Chase." I fought the sense of defeat creeping up on me...and failed miserably. "Sooner or later, the truth will come out, you know that. What happens then?"

"Nothing." He wrapped his arms around my waist and pulled me against his hard chest. The gesture was meant to soothe me, but instead something stirred deep within me, a memory of his hot lips on my skin and exploring fingers between my legs. In spite of the seriousness of the situation, my cheeks caught fire and my breathing accelerated ever so slightly.

"I'll get you the letters," Chase continued, oblivious to the direction my thoughts were taking. "Once you have them, he'll realize you're no threat to his money and he'll stop caring."

"I hope so," I whispered. "I just want him out of my life."

"Then let me deal with him." Chase smiled and his fingers curled beneath my chin, forcing my gaze to meet his. His voice was low and tender as he whispered, "Everything we'll do, we'll do together. As a team. Don't tell anyone about this. The fewer people know, the better." There were faint shadows beneath his eyes, I noticed, but he still looked beautiful. My gaze wandered from his eyes to his mouth and the delicious shadow of a stubble that covered his light bronze skin.

I nodded and moistened my lips, fighting the urge to rub my thumbs against his lower lip and then suck it between my teeth.

"Chase," I said at last, choked on both want and fear. "How can I ever thank you for all you do for me?"

"There's nothing to thank me for."


The End...for now

*An Indecent Proposal: The Interview continues in the sensual sequel,*

# An Indecent

# Proposal:

# The

# agreement

COMING SPRING 2015

# AN INDECENT PROPOSAL BOOK 2:
## THE AGREEMENT
### SNEAK PEEK

PROLOGUE

The first time I saw Lauren Hanson, it was on a snapshot in a thick folder brought to me by my lawyer, Richard Crook. I was sat at the mahogany desk in my multi-million dollar mansion on the outskirts of Santa Barbara in California. The valley stretching beyond the large bay windows was streaked in the colors of the setting sun—the deep red as ominous as the rage surging through me at the prospect of what I was about to do.

Laurie was an attractive girl with brown hair reaching down to her narrow waist—the kind you could twist around your fist and pull gently as you rode her hard, then forget all about her. She looked like a nice girl with an innocent glint in her hazel eyes that reflected even through a photograph. In less than forty-eight hours I'd be using that innocence to make her mine forever.

"Are you sure, Mr. Wright?" Crook asked.

I nodded gravely and tossed the folder back to him.

"You've barely looked at her," he continued, "or her background. Maybe you should wait. I could look into alternatives and…"

"I'm not interested in her life story," I said through gritted teeth, cutting him off. "Just make that meeting happen, and I'll take over from there."

Crook heaved a defeated sigh. He didn't argue as he picked up the folder but left Laurie's photo on the desk. Her hazel gaze looked at me accusingly. I turned it over so I could flee it for the time being, figuring soon enough I'd have no choice but to face the hatred embedded in her eyes, staining her heart forever.

"Tomorrow afternoon," Crook said upon leaving. "If you change your mind…"

"I won't," I said sharply, "and don't be late."


\*\*\*End of Excerpt\*\*\*


Find out Chase Wright's secret.

An Indecent Proposal: The Agreement will be out in Spring 2015. Please join our mailing list to be notified of the release:

*http://jcreedauthor.blogspot.com/p/mailing-list.html*

*http://authorjackiesteele.blogspot.com/p/subscribe.html*

If you enjoyed this book, please leave a review, as they are hard to come by for indie authors. And finally, don't be a stranger. We love to hear from our readers and always write back. To contact us, visit the blogs above or join us on Facebook (links are on the next page.)

## ABOUT THE AUTHORS

Jackie S. Steele has lived most of her life in New England. She never read a book she didn't like. Her love for books began when she stumbled upon her mother's secret dash of Harlequin books, and couldn't stop reading until she had finished them all. Today she still loves curling up with a good book, sipping coffee, and taking long walks on the beach.

http://www.facebook.com/AuthorJackieSteele

http://jackiesteele.wix.com/main

J.C. Reed is the New York Times, Wall Street Journal and USA Today bestselling author of SURRENDER YOUR LOVE and CONQUER YOUR LOVE. She writes steamy contemporary fiction with a touch of mystery. When she's not typing away on her keyboard, forgetting the world around her, she dreams of returning to the beautiful mountains of Wyoming. You can also find her chatting on Facebook with her readers or spending time with her three children.

https://www.facebook.com/AuthorJCReed

http://jcreedauthor.blogspot.com

BOOKS BY J.C. REED:

SURRENDER YOUR LOVE

CONQUER YOUR LOVE

TREASURE YOUR LOVE

THE LOVER'S SECRET

THE LOVER'S GAME

THE LOVER'S PROMISE

THE LOVER'S SURRENDER…coming soon.

THAT GUY

AN INDECENT PROPOSAL: THE INTERVIEW

AN INDECENT PROPOSAL: THE AGREEMENT


BOOKS BY JACKIE STEELE:

THAT GUY

AN INDECENT PROPOSAL: THE INTERVIEW

AN INDECENT PROPOSAL: THE *AGREEMENT*

Made in the USA
Middletown, DE
18 June 2015